DEM BONES, DEM BONES

SPELLBOUND HOUND MAGIC AND MYSTERY BOOK 5

JEANNIE WYCHERLEY

Dem Bones, Dem Bones
Spellbound Hound Magic and Mystery Book 5
BY

JEANNIE WYCHERLEY

Bark at the Moon Books

Sign up for Jeannie's newsletter:
www.subscribepage.com/JeannieWycherleyWonky

Dem Bones, Dem Bones was edited by Christine L Baker
Cover design by Cover Affairs.

Formatting by Tammy
Proofreading by Johnny Bon Bon

Please note: This book is set in England in the United Kingdom. It uses British English spellings and idioms.

This episode of Toby's amazing spellbound adventures is dedicated to my very own 'Old Pete' and his devoted Yorkie, Sparky.

Peter Alderson Sharp, Dad, this one is for you.
Your loving daughter
Jeannie Wycherley
14th December 2023

CHAPTER ONE

Toby was minding his own business.

That is to say, he was minding his business by taking a keen, personal interest in it. He lay sprawled on the rug in frog pose, the local newspaper spread out in front of him, studying the classified ads. Occasionally, he would spot something he liked and his tail would thump the floor. In the gold light of the setting sun, the resulting specks of dust wafted around by his sudden enthusiasm sparkled and glinted most pleasingly. Pleasing that is unless, like Clarissa, you were reminded of the pressing need to do some housework.

Toby, a schnauzer-collie-whippet-terrier-thingie, didn't particularly care about such mundane activity. In fact, he tended to find the whole procedure rather annoying. It wasn't just the pointless movement of dust around from one area to another; it was also the need to get the noisy monster with the long rubbery tentacle and greedy mouth out from under the stairs and let it roar its way around the house. It went everywhere! Such an imposition on Toby's privacy, and horrendously LOUD!

And annoying!

However, Clarissa, Toby's human, insisted on a certain measure of cleanliness in the house. As young as she was—she claimed to be in her twenties, although this sounded absurdly old to Toby—she frequently informed Toby that she had STANDARDS and that keeping house was a RESPONSIBILITY she didn't take lightly.

Toby had been working on his reading and writing and spelling—he was less fond of arithmetic, but Mrs Crouch next door had been trying to demonstrate multiplication and division using dog treats as a visual aid—and he often spelled out important words in his head for practice and capitalised the ones he wanted to remember.

What escaped his understanding was why Clarissa, a witch, couldn't just clean the house using magick. If it had been down to him, Toby certainly would have done. It would make life so much easier to intone a few words and whisk the mess away and, as a result, he and Clarissa would enjoy more time to play together or take long walks around the park. This would have been appreciated by them both, Toby was certain of that. Clarissa, a contributing journalist to *The Celestine Times* for the south-west region, often worked long hours. If a story broke at teatime, Toby would find himself postponing his evening walk—sometimes indefinitely—and crossing his legs as she began to type frantically on her laptop while simultaneously fielding phone calls from her editor and fellow journalists. He might whine, throw her a little side-eye, but she had grown adept at ignoring his petulance, and eventually he'd either have to take himself for a little meander around the neighbourhood—something Clarissa hated him doing—or simply relieve himself in his own garden.

Oh, the horror!

She might have a responsibility to the house—the one they'd inherited from Toby's first owner and Clarissa's grandad, Old Joe—but Toby had a responsibility to the garden and the diverse ecosystem within it. What would the birds and the bees, and everything in between, think of him doing what doggies need to do ... in the middle of their *homes*?

Bees can be hideously judgemental.

Far better for Toby to take it out and about around the neighbourhood. This had the added advantage of allowing him to check for pee-mails, such a vital communication tool for any hound.

Especially *spellbound* hounds.

Toby had been a magickal dog—spellbound—ever since Old Joe had clapped eyes on him. The old man had cast a spell that allowed Toby to converse with witches and wizards. Toby also had the ability to learn far more than 'normal' dogs—some of whom struggled with sit and stay, let alone anything more complicated than that, although to be fair, Toby wasn't that great at staying unless he chose to, and frequently he didn't—including, it had transpired, magick.

There were two things Toby desired in life.

Wait. Make that three.

Firstly, he wanted to find The Pointy Woman and bring her to justice. Secondly, he wanted to become a great wizard. Eventually he hoped he'd be capable of casting magnificent spells and writing magickal books, and he would generally astonish the world.

And thirdly, he wanted a constant supply of sammiches.

This evening, while Clarissa provided the background soundtrack of tippity-tapping on her keyboard with the occasional thought whispered out loud or a couple of tuts and frantic backspaces, Toby was working on the second of those desires.

Number three was an ongoing grumble in his tummy.

He cocked his head and peered more closely at a small square of words in the centre of the fourth column. His pen, a suitably magickal, purple-coloured Staedtler marker, hovered in the air, ready to pounce.

Free to Collector, Toby read. *Garden shed in good condition. 8 by 6. Room required. Need gone now.*

He took a moment to chew over the words. In the absence of sammiches, chewing over words was the next best thing to do. *Free to Collector*. What did that mean? Toby wasn't a collector of garden sheds. Did that mean it wouldn't be free to him? Would he have to pay? If so, how much?

"Clarissa?" He peered over his shoulder.

"Mmm?" Clarissa paused but kept her focus on the screen.

"How much money do I have?"

Now she did turn her head to regard him, almost quizzically. "What do you mean, how much money do *you* have?"

Toby reconsidered the words he'd used. *Yep.* They seemed right to him. He spoke more slowly so that Clarissa, bless her, could understand him more easily. "How much money, m-o-n-e-y, money do I have?"

Clarissa huffed and shook her head, turning her attention back to her screen. "Toby, you don't have any money. You're a dog."

Toby gasped and jumped up, rounding on Clarissa in dismay. "Surely there must be some mistake?"

"That you're a dog? Nope. No mistake." Clarissa began tapping again. "Bah! Only in my spelling."

Hurrying over, Toby climbed onto the chair beside her to get a better look at what she was writing. "I know this one! It's l-e-i-s-u-r-e-l-y—" he managed, before she pushed him away.

"I know!" She rolled her eyes at him.

"Why is it underlined then?" he asked, struggling to stay on his chair.

"It's a typo." She nodded at him. "Why do you want to know about money you don't have?"

"I've been working on a business proposition for some time," Toby told her, "and I think I may have located some premises."

Clarissa frowned. "Come again?"

"Look!" He bounced down to the floor and skidded over to the rug, rucking it up as he did so and sending more glittering specks into the atmosphere. "See here."

The purple pen dropped onto the page Toby had been reading and neatly circled the advert.

Reluctantly, Clarissa slid from her seat and came over to crouch beside Toby.

"Free to Collector—" she read.

"I don't know why anyone would collect sheds," Toby told her. "I'm not a collector, and it doesn't say how much a non-collector would have to pay—"

"It probably means free to the person who collects it," Clarissa told him. "The person who picks it up."

"Wow! You'd have to be strong to pick up a shed."

"Not literally, you daft dog. The person who takes the shed away!" Clarissa elbowed him and read on.

"Oh." Toby hadn't thought of that. The nuances of the English language could escape him sometimes.

"In good condition?" Clarissa reached out and stroked Toby's head. "We've already got a shed, Tobes!"

"But it's full of stuff!" Toby complained.

"That's what they're for. To store things."

"I need an empty shed."

Clarissa resumed reading. "Eight by six—"

"That's the size. In feet," Toby told her, full of knowledge he wished to share.

Clarissa tutted. "I know what eight by six means, Toby." Shaking her head, she continued. "Room required. Need gone now. Oh! I hate that expression. *Need gone now*! Ugh! Ugh!"

Toby patted the page, his face solemn. "What do you think?"

"I told you what I think. We already have a shed."

"But—"

"It's full of stuff. I know. You said." Clarissa raised her eyebrows. "Spill the beans. Why do you want to use the shed?"

"I don't want to use *the* shed. *The* shed is full of stuff. Stuff that keeps the garden in tip-top condition and is therefore vitally important!" Toby liked to think of himself as the champion or hero the garden needed. Clarissa wasn't particularly green-fingered—although she tried her best, and it could be said she had improved since they'd first moved in. Mrs Crouch, their witchy neighbour, often passed on tips and occasionally took it upon herself to tend the front garden when Clarissa wasn't looking. Mrs Crouch had a bee-autiful garden. "I need my *own* shed."

"You want a whole shed to yourself?" Clarissa scratched her head. "Do you want to use it as a kennel?"

Toby gasped. "Take that word out of your mouth!"

"Sorry! Sorry!" Clarissa raised her hands in alarm.

Toby shivered. He hated the word 'kennel' as

much as he loathed the word 'pound'. You might as well have substituted either of those for prison. It meant *exactly* the same thing.

"Do you want to ..." Clarissa rephrased her original query, "live out in the garden? I know how fond you are of it."

"Good grief, no." Toby reeled at the idea. "I'm not an outdoorsy type of dog. I like my home comforts too much." He indicated his fat squidgy basket in front of the television, covered in a sheepskin rug. He had his own cushion, too. *A Spoiled Dog Sleeps Here*, it said in blue gingham on cream calico. This was partly true and partly a lie. He napped in his basket during the day, but overnight he actually slept on a blanket on Old Joe's bed. It allowed him to feel closer to the dearly departed, kindly old man he'd loved so much.

No, Toby was in no hurry to sleep outside in a shed.

"I told you. It's for my business."

Clarissa sank backwards, pulling her legs underneath her to sit cross-legged. Perhaps she had a feeling that this conversation might take a little more of her time than she'd anticipated.

"Tell me about your business, Tobes," she said.

Arranging himself neatly in front of her, paws together, Toby grinned, pleased he had her full attention. "Initially it would be more of a studio, I suppose," he said. "Somewhere I can learn and experiment at the same time. But in due course—quite soon, I would anticipate—I'd like to accept clients—"

Clarissa's eyebrows disappeared into her hairline. This wasn't difficult because, although she had taken to wearing her hair in four quirky bunches on the sides of her head, she allowed her floppy fringe to fall around her eyes. Face-framing, she called it.

Toby ignored her reaction. "I'll perform magick spells, maybe do a little investigative work, offer counselling and magickal advice, that kind of thing. It will become a kind of studio-come-office for Toby Silverwind Enterprises incorporating Spellbound Investigative Services."

Clarissa opened her mouth, closed it again, fought to keep a straight face, then gave up and guffawed.

If Toby had been able to, he would have pouted. Being a dog, pouting proved impossible, so he glared at his human instead. That only made matters worse.

"Hahaha!" Clarissa clutched at her stomach, fighting for breath.

Toby, unimpressed, stretched his head back and stared at the ceiling. There were cobwebs up there. He found spiders fascinating. One of them was staring down at Clarissa, all of its eyes wide with trepidation, probably wondering what all the noise was about.

"Have you finished?" Toby asked, when Clarissa had finally wound down.

"Suh-suh-sorry!" Clarissa hiccupped, regarding her hound with what Toby took to be a mix of bewilderment and affection. "Are you ..." She drew in a shuddering breath. "Are you totally serious?"

"Totally."

"Totally totally?"

Toby nodded. "Totally totally totally. It's going to be my wizard's shack."

Clarissa sighed. "Even if we enquire about it, I'm not sure we'd manage to carry a shed in our car. It's a bit small."

Toby primped himself. *Winner, winner, sammich for dinner*! Clarissa could never say no to him. "I know a man who can!" he told her.

Time to place a call to Not-so-dead-to-me Ed.

CHAPTER TWO

Toby was supervising.

He'd assumed he would be supervising the loading of chunks of shed into the back of Detective Ed's shiny new four-by-four truck thingie. It was one of those with a flatbed and a lid—a lid he'd left behind on Clarissa's driveway—and Ed was entranced by it in a way that men with shiny new toys often are.

However, when Toby, Ed and Clarissa had rolled up at the shed seller's address—an ugly, squat, pebble-dashed bungalow with a wraparound garden—it had quickly become apparent that the shed was still shed-shaped rather than flat-packed.

Clarissa exchanged a grimace with Ed as the front door opened and a man in his late twenties or early thirties, with shoulder-length floppy brown hair and wearing paint-spattered dungarees and a terracotta jumper full of holes, loped out to meet them.

"Hey," he said.

"Hi." Clarissa held out a hand. "I'm Clarissa. We spoke on the phone."

"Enchanté," said the young man, without the slightest hint of a French accent. He held onto Clarissa's hand just a little longer than was necessary. Toby and Ed eyed him with equal suspicion. "I'm Connor Riseby."

"Pleased to meet you," Clarissa said. "This is my friend, Ed."

Connor gave Ed a quick up and down before shaking his hand. "Ed."

"And this is Toby," Clarissa finished.

"Hey, scrumptious!" Connor reached down and scruggled Toby's head.

"Watch it, Buster!" Toby shook himself. Today he *wasn't* okay with people he'd never met getting overly familiar with him.

"Cute fella." Connor stood and smiled at Clarissa, angling himself so he was slightly edging Ed out of the conversation. "Vocal too."

"Yes," Clarissa agreed. "A little too much at times." She pointed at the shed. "Is this the one you advertised?"

Toby harrumphed. *Well, der! Can you see any other?*

"Yes. I bought this place about two months ago and I'm gradually doing it up. I've decided to take the shed down and put a carport in its place." He shrugged. "I can't afford a garage."

"You've bought this for yourself?" Clarissa asked.

"Nah. I'm going to rent it out. You can make a fortune around here with rentals." He winked. "Starting a property empire, I am."

"Impressive," Clarissa said.

Ed sniffed. Toby had the distinct impression Ed wasn't impressed by Connor's entrepreneurial spirit. Or maybe it was his good looks ... or the way he was flirting with Clarissa ...

"We thought the shed would be ready to go," Ed said. "And we'd just be loading it ..."

"I'm so sorry," the shed seller apologised, pointing at the still-erect shed. "I haven't been awake long."

"Really?" Ed asked, glancing pointedly at his watch. He'd just come off a late-running nightshift and had therefore been at work for twenty hours before pulling up in front of Clarissa's house in need of a shower, a shave and a good meal. He'd had none of those because Toby had jollied them all along and given them no peace until they'd clambered into Ed's posh truck.

Clarissa smiled. "Not a problem," she said. "We'll help you take it down. Won't we, Ed?"

"Sure," said Ed, sounding less than keen.

"Can I fix you a drink or anything?" Connor dragged a hand through his locks, tossing his fringe—suggestively, Toby thought—while leering at Clarissa.

"We're fine," said Ed.

Oooh, no. Mistake. Toby placed his paw carefully on the toe of Ed's boot and applied a little pressure. "I wouldn't answer for Clarissa if I were you," Toby told him, not that the detective could understand what he was saying. "She doesn't like it ..."

"Some water for Toby would be great," Clarissa said, shooting Ed an evil glare. "It's a hot day."

Connor nodded. Opening the shed door, he pulled out a number of tools lying on the floor waiting to be put to use. A hammer, a pair of screwdrivers and a crowbar. "Do you want to get started, Ed? Do you know how to use these? I'll be right back to give you a hand. I'll just get the puppy some water."

Puppy? Toby bristled. *The absolute cheek of the man.*

Connor handed the tools over, accidentally—perhaps—dropping the screwdrivers at Ed's feet.

"Oops. Soz!" Turning to Clarissa, Connor indicated the open front door. "Would you like to see what I've managed to do so far?"

"Ooh, yes. I love a bit of home improvement ..." Their voices trailed off as the pair disappeared inside.

Toby gazed up at Ed, the detective clutching the crowbar in one hand and the hammer in the other.

Ed stared back at him, his face flushed. "Do I know how to use these?" he muttered. "If he had the merest inkling of the crime scenes I've visited and knew how many ways I've seen the results of these items when they've been put to nefarious uses ... If he understood the damage they can do to flesh, he wouldn't be asking me that!"

"Steady, Ed," said Toby. "I hear that coppers don't do well on the inside."

Ed blew his cheeks out. "Stand out of the way, Toby, I don't want you getting hurt."

Toby moved to a triangular patch of shadow against the external wall of the bungalow. The sun beat down on the dried-out garden. There might have been plants and bushes here once, but the lawn had turned brown with lack of water, and any shrubbery had long since been pulled up or rotted away.

Ed started with the shed door, whacking the

uppermost hinge when he couldn't get the screw to turn.

"Ed, Ed, Ed, my boy!" Toby interjected. "That's my new wizard shack!"

Ed cast a sideways glance at him. "I could swear you're trying to give me directions ..."

"I am!" Toby told him. "And you *shouldn't* swear because it's not nice. So don't."

Clarissa and Connor came out of the bungalow at that moment, Clarissa clutching a glass of juice in one hand and a soup bowl in the other. She and Connor were giggling together.

"It'll be lovely when it's finished," she was saying. She placed the soup bowl in front of Toby. He glared suspiciously at the contents and sniffed derisively. Definitely water. But for all he knew, it might be *toxic* water. A dog could never be too careful.

He turned his head away.

"Fussy bum," Clarissa hissed.

"It's probably got turps and paint in it and wood-chip shavings for all I know," Toby complained.

"Of course it hasn't." Shaking her head, Clarissa left Toby to it.

In this case, as far as Toby was concerned, 'it' meant supervising the dismantling of the shed and loading it into Ed's new monster truck, but as the afternoon progressed, it became more of a supervision of the battle of testosterone between Ed and Connor. Toby lay on his belly, panting like a steam train, dying for a slurp of water but refusing to give in and drink from the soup bowl, while Connor—evidently a sun worshipper judging by his tan—stripped off his jumper, tied the dungaree cords low over his abdomen and showed off his six-pack. Connor worked quickly and efficiently to remove nails and screws, while Ed huffed and swore and sweated through his work shirt, tools and nails and screws dropping out of his sweaty, slippery grasp.

"We should keep the screws, Ed," Clarissa suggested after the fourth time she'd had to drop to her knees and crawl around hunting for one he'd dropped.

"I know!" Ed puffed.

"Don't you worry, I have loads." Connor laughed. "I can send you home with a few spares."

"That's so kind of you," Clarissa said. "I'm sure we can pick some up from the DIY place."

"It's no bother, honestly. I have more than I'll ever need." Connor grinned. "Until my next project, of course."

"You'll be a millionaire before you know it," Clarissa said.

"That's the plan!"

Ed sniffed.

Toby regarded the poor detective with interest. His flushed face and the set of his jaw suggested Ed might be feeling a little antagonistic towards the budding property developer. Jealous, Toby surmised.

Toby left the sanctity of his minuscule triangle of shade and trotted over to Ed. Standing alongside him as the detective wheezed and perspired, Toby nudged his calf. "You don't need to be jealous," he told him. "Clarissa learned her lesson last time. She won't fall for this guy's baloney."

Ed glanced at Toby. "Are you hot?" he asked. "Go back in the shade. We won't be long." Turning to Clarissa, he said, "Maybe we should have left Toby at home?"

"It is a bit warm for him," she agreed.

"Oh, do you guys share a house, then?" Connor asked, looking from one to the other.

"No, no," Clarissa was quick to say.

"Oh." Connor's eyes lit up. "I just thought because Ted was talking about home—"

"It's Ed," Ed replied, a little testily. "Or DC Plum if you prefer."

"He meant Toby's home," Clarissa said, jumping in to cover the sudden awkwardness.

"Old Joe's home, as was," Toby informed Connor.

"Now it's mine and Clarissa's." He wrinkled his nose at Connor. "And *nobody* else's."

"I see." Connor removed yet another nail. "Right, I think the roof is ready to come off—"

"Let me help you." Clarissa moved to stand next to Connor.

"Don't you dare," said Ed, crossly. "You've only been out of that cast a few weeks!"

"I'm fine!" Clarissa protested.

Ed was adamant. "Absolutely not!"

Clarissa sighed. "Sorry, Connor. It's why I asked Ed to help. I broke my leg a little while ago. I'm not supposed to do too much weight-bearing until my GP signs me off."

"Ah, I see. Sorry to hear that!" Connor sympathised. "It must make life difficult. Don't you worry. Big Ted and I have got this! Haven't we, Ted?"

Ooo-er. Toby's eyes were wide. Ed looked as though he might explode out of his shirt any moment, but Clarissa placed a hand on the detective's arm and he simmered down immediately.

"Ed's my hero," she said, and all Ed's angst and frustration swiftly evaporated.

After that, Connor and Ed worked together more effectively, although Ed still had what Old Joe would have called buttery fingers. Toby had often wondered about this expression. Neither Old Joe nor Ed had fingers made of dairy products, but it was true that both of them had a tendency to drop things. Especially when they were tired.

Finally the shed was down and the men began moving the pieces onto Ed's truck.

"Gently! Gently!" Toby instructed. "Don't damage it!" And, "Careful now! That's an integral part of my shack!" until Connor began to look a little rattled by his constant interventions.

"Sssh," Clarissa told him, but Toby faced up to her.

"This is my future!" he reminded her. "My business empire starts here."

"Spirits protect us," she muttered.

"I'll certainly make enquiries of them when I reach that stage of my learning," Toby agreed, although ghost whispering was advanced stuff that he wouldn't be learning for a year or two yet.

Once every component of the shed had been loaded onto the truck, and Connor had handed over two bags—one with screws and the other with shiny new nails—Clarissa shook his hand. "Thanks so much, Connor. We truly appreciate it. Don't we, Toby?"

"Yes, we do. Thank you." Toby liked to be seen to be well-mannered. Plus, it had been a fun afternoon in some ways—entertaining, at least—and he'd never have to see Connor again, which was a bonus. He could afford to be magnanimous.

"Cheers, mate," said Ed, also holding out his hand. His good humour appeared to have been restored too, now that their departure was imminent.

"You know?" Connor held up a finger. "Perhaps I should come back with you and help you put the shed up?"

"Oh, that's really not necessary!" Clarissa protested.

"Absolutely not," said Toby.

"We'll be fine," Ed agreed.

"But you said yourself that Clarissa shouldn't be weight-bearing, and honestly? It's no skin off my nose. I'll only be doing some more painting if I stay here."

Toby looked at Ed, waiting to see what he'd say. "I ... er ... oh. I didn't think we were going to be putting it up ... Oh." Ed didn't seem to know how to respond.

"It's a lovely day. I'd rather be outside than inside painting skirting boards," Connor admitted.

Ed glanced at Clarissa. She grimaced. "The thing is, Connor, Ed's just come off a nightshift," she explained. "He's a little tired—"

"Oh, I see." Connor nodded, his face creased with sympathy.

"No, you're right," Ed relented. "We should make

hay while the sun shines and build the shed this afternoon."

"Are you sure?" Clarissa double-checked.

"Absolutely. Let's go." Ed turned for his truck, fishing in his trouser pocket for the keys. Only Toby caught his look of pure exasperation.

Not-so-dead-to-me Ed is jealous, Toby realised. *He wants Clarissa all to himself.*

CHAPTER THREE

"Is it a little bit ... crooked?" Moriarty, the cat from across the road, cocked her head one way and then the other.

"Do you think it is?" Toby scrutinised the shed, trying to see it through her eyes.

Pippin, Toby's best friend, scratched behind her ear. There was every chance she had fleas. As a stray, she lived mainly on the streets, scrounging for her dinners. Her coat, generally light cream and grey, was caked with dust from where she'd been sleeping rough. They hadn't had any rain in this part of Devon recently, and poor old Pippin hadn't been able to wash. "Looks okay to me," she said.

Toby grabbed the piece of lined A4 paper he'd ripped out of one of Clarissa's notepads. "It's certainly coming along." He dabbed a paw at his drawing. "The porthole has to go in here. See? That will give me a little light so I can see what I'm doing until I get electricity installed."

"Ooh, posh," ventured Moriarty. "Electy-ricity, eh? All mod cons."

"You'd better believe it." He pointed at the right-hand side of the shed. "And I'm going to get a ladder to put up here—"

"Where are you going to get a ladder from?" Pippin asked.

"There's one at the side of the house. It's the one Clarissa tripped over when she broke her leg. She'll be glad to see the back of it, trust me." Toby nodded knowingly.

"She'll still see it if it's attached to a shed in her garden," Moriarty pointed out.

"True." Toby hadn't thought of that. "Maybe I can disguise it somehow." He waved a paw at the drawing, and some green squiggly lines wrapped themselves around the ladder illustration. "Vines or something. Ivy? Clematis …? Hmmm."

"Why do you want a ladder, anyway?" Moriarty asked. "Are you planning to sunbathe?"

"Goodness, no. You cats are weird."

Pippin nodded. "True, that."

Moriarty curled her lip. "At least I don't need a ladder to get on a shed roof."

"Touché," said Pippin.

Toby decided to rise above this. "I figure, if I can get a little higher, I'll be able to tune into the Twilight Barking without having to go to the park."

Now Pippin and Moriarty were looking at him with admiration. "Genius!" muttered Pippin.

"Exactly!" said Toby. "More and more often Clarissa is working, and so I miss my evening walk. Now I won't need to bother her. I'll just come out here and climb up the ladder, settle myself down with some snacks and tune in." The snacks were an essential part of this scenario, of course.

"Mega!" said Moriarty. "I might come and join you."

"Cats don't do the Twilight Barking," Pippin grumbled.

"But you're welcome anytime," Toby hurriedly chipped in. He didn't want his friends falling out. "I'll get some cat treats in." He was certain Mrs Crouch would help him with that.

"When will the porthole go in?" Pippin asked.

"Clarissa said she'd do that once the shed's been painted." Toby frowned.

"And when will that be?" Moriarty asked.

"There's the thing. DC Ed is going to paint the shed. He promised. I think he was trying to get on Clarissa's good side."

Moriarty's eyes glinted. "Did that work?"

"Who knows?" Toby shrugged. "I don't understand what's going on with those two. One minute they're friends and giggling like school kids, and the next they're a bit"—he screwed up his face, trying to think what they were a bit of—"wibbly wobbly."

"Wibbly wobbly?" Pippin repeated.

"Like the shed, you mean?" Moriarty asked.

Toby blinked at her. "The shed is *fine*!"

She backed off, elegantly lifting a paw and proceeding to lick it with small, precise movements. "Just saying."

Toby ignored her. "My point is, I have no idea when the shed will be painted because they didn't set a date, and like most hoomans they're both always too *busy*." Toby groaned. "I'll never understand why hoomans want to be busy constantly. They should make more time in life for the important things. Eating and sleeping!"

Moriarty started on her other paw. "Watching the world go by."

"Sitting outside the butcher's shop on Draper's Row and waiting for some scraps," Pippin said.

"And painting sheds!" Toby finished. "I mean, priorities!"

"You could do it yourself, of course," Pippin suggested. "Why wait, right?"

"Do it myself?" Toby repeated, ready to poo-poo the idea, but even as the words escaped his mouth, he experienced a surge of excitement. *Do it myself! Why not?* There was paint in the other shed. Old Joe had stored pots of it for years. There were brushes and spongey paint-implement-tool-type things and paint trays and all manner of paraphernalia. All he needed to do was root them out.

"That's a great idea!" He yipped with excitement, so loudly that Clarissa came to the back door.

She stuck her head outside, blinking into the sunshine like a myopic owl. "What are you up to?"

"Nothing," Toby said, wishing he could whistle nonchalantly, but have you ever heard a dog whistle? No. And you won't. Why? Because they can't make the necessary shape with their mouths. And also, if they could, they'd be whistling to each other in the parks and forests and on the streets and beaches, and no owner would ever get the right dog to come back. "Nothing at all."

"Hmmm." Clarissa narrowed her eyes.

"Nothing to see here," Toby added, channelling his inner Obi-Wan Kenobi. "Move along."

"Just stay out of trouble, okay?" Clarissa ordered and, without waiting for an answer, returned to whatever news article she was in the process of researching.

"As if I'd *ever* get into trouble," Toby said to the closed back door before jerking his head at Old Joe's shed. "Right, ladies! Let's grab what we need."

"Have you ever painted anything before?" Moriarty asked, sniffing the lids on the tins of paint.

"Mmmm, not exactly," said Toby.

"What does 'not exactly' mean?" asked Pippin, nuzzling the spongey rolling-pin thingies.

"It means no," Moriarty translated helpfully.

Toby pawed at the paint trays. "How difficult can it be?"

"I think we're about to find out." Moriarty climbed onto the biggest pot of paint. "What about this one?"

"What colour is it?" Toby asked.

"Some kind of blue, judging by the spillage on the side of the tin," said Moriarty.

Toby took a closer look. "Meadow Fresh Bluebell," he read. "Why do paints have such silly names?"

"I like blue," said Pippin.

"I was hoping to paint the shed green so it would blend with its surroundings, though," Toby said, taking a look at the labels on the smaller pots. Custard Crème. Walnut Whip. Chocolate Bomb. Japanese Cherry Tree. Snowflake. Sandstorm. Peach Melba. Not a hint of green. *Dog in heaven*! "I'm not sure whether you're supposed to paint with some of these or cook with them instead," Toby said. "Let's have a look at the blue." Levitating a screwdriver, he inserted it beneath the lid with a bit of oomph and, after a few goes, he finally managed to prise the lid off, although not without splashing his beard and swallowing a little too.

Bleugh! "Definitely not for cooking with."

The three of them craned forward to take a better look at the colour. It *was* reminiscent of bluebells—there could be little doubt about that.

"That's the colour in the spare bedroom," Toby said. "Old Joe only used it on one of the walls."

"He must have changed his mind," said Moriarty.

"There's wallpaper on the other three walls." Toby shrugged. "I think it was a decorating choice. What do we make of it? Is it a wizardly colour?" An element of doubt had crept into his voice.

"I don't mind it," Pippin said.

"Mmm." Moriarty wasn't convinced.

"The way I see it, it's this or nothing," said Pippin. "Because you don't have enough of any of the others."

"That's a good point." Toby stole a quick look at the back door, wondering how receptive Clarissa might be to providing him with more paint. Probably not very.

"Let's do it!" he said and reached for a paint tray.

Forty minutes later, Toby stood back to survey their work in progress. Pippin dropped the sizable paint-brush she'd been wielding in her mouth and panted. Moriarty, equipped only with an artist's brush, had been filling in a small square on the barge boards that surrounded the roof. She claimed not to be able to handle a brush any bigger than that. To be fair, her square of paint was the neatest by far.

Pippin hadn't a scooby about painting. Not. A. Single. Clue. She'd dipped her brush into the paint pot and then flourished it with wild abandon, sending paint here, there and everywhere, pebble-dashing the door to great effect. She'd tried to reach the upper part of the shed by standing on her hind legs and resting her paws on the wall to help support her weight. She couldn't quite stretch up to the top but had left an artistic array of paw prints all around two walls.

Toby had been using the spongey rolling-pin thingie. This gave better coverage, to be sure, but he'd been overly lavish with the paint to begin with, meaning it had puckered up and taken on an artexed effect. As the amount of paint dwindled, he was forced to become much stingier with its use. Without enough paint on the roller, halfway around the shed, the wood began to adopt a distressed appearance.

But not half as distressed as Clarissa when she came out to see why Toby was so quiet. She hadn't expected that the reason for her peace was because he had a paint roller stuffed in his gob.

"Toby!" Clarissa shrieked, startling both dogs and Moriarty, who scrambled to keep her balance on the roof, *and* simultaneously alerting Mrs Crouch, who was in her own garden.

The elderly neighbour popped her head over the fence. "Everything alright?" she asked, but did a double take when she spotted the shed. "Oh my."

"What do you think you're doing?" Clarissa asked, stomping up the garden towards Toby and his friends.

"Painting," said Toby. *Obvs.*

"But ... but ..." Clarissa gestured around. "Ed said he'd do it."

Toby cleared his throat. It seemed to be gummed up with Meadow Fresh Bluebell paint. "With all due respect to Ed, I couldn't wait that long."

"You couldn't wait ...?" Clarissa choked, met Mrs Crouch's eye and shook her head, lost for words.

"You have to admit it's artistic," Mrs Crouch suggested.

Toby preened.

"Although I'm not sure what the Royal Horticultural Society would think of it," she continued.

"I think they'd probably bomb it from space," Clarissa replied, her voice faint. "Nuke it!"

Toby sulked. "It's not that bad." He stepped back to get a better look. The paint strokes went this way and that, willy-nilly, barely covering the wood in some places, saturating it in others. Pippin's paw prints circled two sides, much like a garland, while Moriarty's small, neat square sat alone on the finial.

Worse than all of this, perhaps, was the fact that the bushes and plants surrounding the shed—late summer foliage—had been spattered with blue paint, as had the bird feeder and bird bath and—oopsie—Clarissa's smalls, which she'd hung on the washing line first thing this morning.

Toby hadn't noticed them there. *Zero out of ten for observation.*

He swallowed. "I mean, it's not that bad for a first attempt."

Clarissa stared at him.

Toby offered her a teeny wag. Just the tip of his tail.

"It's like a scene from a dystopian Alice in Wonderland," Clarissa whispered.

"Maybe the rain will wash it off?" he suggested, mentally crossing his paws.

"And will the rain wash you off?" Clarissa asked.

Toby inspected himself. His blue chest and front paws. *Oh dear*. He turned his head. *Yoikes*. He had blue spots all over his back, like some surrealist Dalmatian. Albeit a short and hairy one.

Clarissa pivoted and marched back to the house. Toby imagined she would get a bucket of warm, soapy water and give him a bath, but she slammed the door, which he took as her final comment on the matter.

Would the rain wash him off? It would eventually —if she never let him in the house again!

Mrs Crouch wheezed. Pippin and Toby turned to her in alarm, but she was only struggling to keep her mirth inside. Now that Clarissa had disappeared, she gave rein to it, erupting and braying like a donkey on laughing gas.

Pippin met Toby's eye. He shrugged, noticing that

now the paint was drying, his coat had started to stiffen up. If he didn't get a barf sometime soon, he'd be frozen into place for eternity. Pippin was in a worse state than him, but being Pippin, she didn't seem to care much.

"Mrs Crouch?" Toby asked when his neighbour took a breather.

Struggling to contain herself, she wiped the tears from her cheeks. "Yes, Toby?"

"What would you do?" The words came out sounding more woebegone than he'd intended. Painting the shed had seemed like an excellent idea at the time, but having seen Clarissa's reaction, he wasn't so sure.

Mrs Crouch smiled at him. "Sometimes, Toby, you just have to fully commit to something."

"Finish what you've started, you mean?" he asked.

"That's exactly what I mean."

CHAPTER FOUR

The sun had sunk low on the horizon. Toby was more exhausted than he'd ever been in his life. Pippin had gone home and now only Moriarty remained, beavering away, painting stars and crescent moons along the shed's fascias, barge boards and overhangs. She'd turned out to be quite the artist. She was especially good at depicting mice and, although Toby wasn't as keen on rodents as she was, he'd allowed her to paint a couple.

The shed was 'finished'.

It didn't look anything like what Toby had had in mind, and part of him felt sad and defeated and annoyed and something of a failure. Of course, they'd run out of Meadow Fresh Bluebell, seeing as most of it had covered them along with Clarissa's plants and pants, and so they'd resorted to using up the rest of the paint from Old Joe's shed. Interestingly, Toby had finally managed to get some green. The Custard Crème—actually more banana than custard, Toby thought—had mixed beautifully with the bluebell and created a kind of grass-green hue. And so here he was, with a shed in alternate colours of blue, green, yellow, peach, pink and chocolate.

"I think I'm done," Moriarty announced. She'd managed, by some miracle, to escape with only a smudge of paint on her cheek. She looked every inch like a proper artist.

"Thanks for all you've done," Toby told her, aware that he looked as though he might as well be auditioning for Joseph and his Technicolour Dreamcoat.

"It's been fun," she said, turning unblinking eyes his way. "I hope your hooman will let you in the house at some stage."

"I'm sure she will," Toby said, forcing a laugh. He wasn't sure at all. If Clarissa had thought the shed had been a mess before, what would she think of it now?

"Catch you later." Moriarty winked and, with one elegant bound, leapt to the nearest tree and disappeared over the back fence.

Left alone, Toby slunk onto his haunches, facing the shed. What had happened to his vision of a wizard's library? A palace of great wisdom overflowing with kindness and benevolence. With its own biscuit tin ...

He heard the back door open behind him and, without looking around, braced himself. Clarissa's footsteps were slow, cautious almost, as she navigated the step up to the garden and the path. *She should be careful*, Toby thought. *We don't want her to break her other leg*.

He almost jumped out of his fur when Clarissa placed a hand on his head. "Hey, you," she said, her voice soft, matching the oncoming twilight.

He turned and gazed up at her, half eager for her love, half scared she would still be mad, but she only smiled at him. She had a plate in her right hand.

"Are you hungry? I brought you out a sammich?" She sat next to him, carefully arranging her leg.

"A little bit." He was *famished*, in fact. "What flavour is it?" Not that it would matter. He'd demolish it, whatever it was.

"Tuna mayonnaise. We don't have much else in."

"That sounds nice." He sniffed at the sandwich, already salivating but feeling awkward. He'd let Clarissa down. She'd wanted something smart in the garden, and all he'd been able to come up with was this catastrophe that might have been a graffitied outhouse on an abandoned railway track.

Clarissa stroked his ears. "I thought this was your favourite?"

"It's not my favourite ..."

"Oh." Clarissa sounded sad.

Toby could bear it no longer. "But it is my favourite favourite!" He could have demolished the sandwich there and then, but he had something more important to do. He crawled onto Clarissa's lap and licked her face. "I'm sorry, Clarissa. I truly am."

"What are you sorry for, you big silly?" She wrapped her arms around him and kissed his forehead, right between his eyes.

"I'm sorry about the shed."

Clarissa gazed at it; her expression unreadable. "It's ... interesting."

"It's a mess," Toby admitted. "It's not what I envij ... envijid ... planned at all."

"Well, why don't you show me what you *envisaged*?" Clarissa asked.

"Really?" Toby wagged his tail in excitement and wriggled out of Clarissa's arms before she could change her mind.

"Of course."

Toby retrieved his paint-spattered plan from

where it languished beneath an empty pot of Peach Melba paint. Old Joe had painted the bathroom with this, but Clarissa wasn't too keen. She'd told Toby she was considering painting the walls red with a black wooden floor and silver accessories. Toby hadn't been sure whether she was joking or not, but Clarissa did favour a goth vibe, so anything was possible.

He smoothed the paper out as best he could, the fur surrounding his middle claw smudging some pale pink paint in the corner. "This is what I wanted."

Clarissa leaned over and studied his drawing. For a dog, it wasn't half bad. "I see the outline of the shed here," she said, tracing it with a finger. "Is this a chimney?"

"Yes. I thought I might find a wood burner or something that would help me to stay warm in the winter."

"So ambitious," said Clarissa, but she didn't sound as though she were mocking him. "And this is ... Are these stairs?"

"Yes," Toby admitted. "But I think I'll have to make do with a ladder."

"I see. And you've covered them in ivy or some other climber?"

Toby bowed his head. "I wanted to make it pretty, Clarissa. So that when you look out of the kitchen window, it doesn't make your eyes sore. Not like this —" He waved a paw at the multicoloured monstrosity before them.

Clarissa chuckled. "I quite like it. It's quirky. But look, we can call what you've done the base coat. We'll talk to Ed, and he can put a top coat on it if you like. I'm sorry. I didn't realise you were in such a rush."

"I was being impatient," Toby admitted. "I could have waited until Ed could do it."

"Knowing Ed, you'd have a long wait," Clarissa said. "His heart is in the right place, but he's a busy man." She ran her finger over the shed roof. "And what's this?"

"It's a platform." This was the part of Toby's architectural genius that he was most excited about. "I can go up there in the evening and listen to the Twilight Barking!"

"Wow." Clarissa raised her eyebrows. "Now that *is* clever." She looked at the shed roof, biting her lip. "That might be beyond Ed's capabilities. It's certainly way beyond mine."

Toby sighed.

Clarissa scrunched his ears. "But never fear. Perhaps ... perhaps we can ask someone else."

Toby wasn't sure whether to be pleased with this or not. He knew she meant Connor. As helpful as

Connor had been thus far—helping Ed reassemble the shed in their back garden and supplying new hinges, nails and screws and even some new floorboards—Toby still felt mistrustful of Clarissa's new friend. For all they knew, he might be a dog snatcher or in league with The Pointy Woman. Had they done their due diligence on this man? No!

Toby, full of sudden cunning, turned on the charm. "If I could have the ladder from the side of the house, perhaps I'd find out I could balance up there without a platform."

"That rotten ladder," Clarissa grumbled. "I suppose ..." She glanced doubtfully at the shed roof again.

"We could try it," Toby urged, aware his impatience was getting the better of him. "If we do it now, I can experiment. If I can hear the Twilight Barking tonight, then we'll know it's an idea worth pursuing."

"True." Clarissa pushed herself carefully to her feet. "I'm not sure I can carry that ladder by myself, but let's see."

"I can help!" Toby trotted after her as she made her way around the side of the house. Since her accident, Ed had tidied along here to make sure there was a clear pathway through. The ladder lay on its side against the wall. At about two yards, it was a perfect height for the shed, but made of wood as it was, it was heavier than a similar one made of aluminium would be.

Clarissa lifted it from the middle and grunted.

"No, no. You take the front, I'll take the rear," said Toby.

"How are you going to take the rear?" Clarissa asked.

"Just lift!" Toby ordered, a tad bossily.

Pulling a face at him, Clarissa did as he asked. At the same time, Toby muttered a levitation spell and his end rose effortlessly.

Clarissa glanced over her shoulder. "Really, Toby? Couldn't you carry the whole thing that way and save me the bother?"

"My magick isn't good enough yet," Toby said, panting with the exertion. "It's a bit heavy for me."

"Quickly then," said Clarissa and moved off towards the garden.

After a little huffing and puffing, on Clarissa's part at least, the pair of them moved the old ladder into position, leaning it against the side wall of the shed.

"It will need properly fastening into place," Clarissa said.

"Can I climb up?" Toby asked. Full darkness

wasn't far away. There were only minutes of the Twilight Barking left.

"I'm not sure how safe it is—"

"If you hold it, I can go up," Toby insisted.

"Just be careful then!" Clarissa footed the ladder with one foot and held it with her right hand. With the opposite hand, she reached down to grab Toby's collar and guide him up the narrow rungs.

Toby had never climbed a ladder before, but he'd seen a stupendously clever dog do so on the telly box. If some random celebrity hound could do it, then so could he! He managed the first couple of rungs easily enough, but then he found that once all four paws were on the ladder, he needed to alter his balance. He'd have preferred the ladder to be sideways on, with a little handrail and the spaces between the rungs filled in, but beggars can't be choosers.

With a wobble and an 'oopsie', and with Clarissa's help, he finally made it to the roof of the shed.

And *yowser*! What a difference a couple of yards made. He could hear the neighbourhood dogs clearly and even make out some distant barking from the area of the park. "This is perfect!" he said.

"Awesome!" said Clarissa. "Would you like to come down now? It doesn't look particularly safe."

"Wait!" Toby cocked his head. He'd thought at first

that the barking was the usual exchange of information he'd expect to hear on any ordinary evening. You know the kind of thing: who'd bitten the postie, who'd had a thermometer poked where the sun doesn't shine, who'd visited the groomer, who'd seen some petty thieves at the marketplace and who'd brought puppies into the world.

But no. Tonight was evidently not an ordinary evening.

To the north, Toby could hear a series of urgent exchanges.

"Top secret!" That was the Great Dane, three streets away. "Calling Toby! Calling Toby!"

"Calling Toby!" The barks and yips echoed all around.

"Has anyone seen Toby?"

"I'm here!" Toby barked back, short and sharp.

"Sssssss!" Clarissa hissed up at him. "You'll disturb the neighbours!"

"Toby?" the Great Dane asked.

"Here!"

"Toby!" Clarissa reached for him.

Toby scuttled backwards, nearly tumbling off the shed. "Hold on, Clarissa!"

"Where have you been?" the Great Dane asked. "We've been trying to reach you."

"Never mind that. What's the message?" Toby barked back.

Clarissa gritted her teeth together. "Uuhh."

"Top secret!" bellowed the Great Dane. "You need to contact Sparky as a matter of urgency."

"Contact Sparky," Toby repeated. "Received."

"Excellent! Over and out!"

And just like that, the Twilight Barking came to an end and the neighbourhood lapsed into silence.

"Who's Sparky?" Clarissa wanted to know.

"He's a remarkably brave Yorkshire terrier I met when I was hunting the puppy snatcher," Toby told her. "Would you mind helping me down, please?"

"Since you asked so nicely." Clarissa reached up and guided him slowly to the bottom of the ladder. "I'm not sure a ladder will work. Not as it is. It isn't safe for you. We'll have to think of something else." She gestured at the back door. "Come on, it's getting late. Let's go in now."

But Toby had other ideas. "I don't suppose—" He turned his chocolate eyes on her, his most beseeching, soul-melting, begging expression ...

Clarissa placed her hands on her hips. "Oh, boy. What do you want now?"

"You wouldn't mind coming for a drive with me?"

"When you say 'coming for a drive', do you actually mean will I drive you somewhere?"

"For you to drive me somewhere, you'd have to be coming with me, wouldn't you?" Toby asked. It seemed clear as day to him.

"Where would we be driving to?"

"Bushy Leaze. It's where Sparky lives."

"Now?" Clarissa glanced at her wrist, but she wasn't wearing a watch so it was a waste of time. "It has to be after half eight. We can't just go knocking on people's doors at this time of night."

"I wouldn't ask if I didn't think it was important," Toby told her.

Clarissa sighed, raising and then dropping her shoulders. "Never a dull moment with you around, is there, babe?"

Toby wagged his tail happily. "Is that a yes?"

"What about your sammich?" Clarissa reached down to pick up the untouched tuna sandwich.

"I'll have it to go, please!"

CHAPTER FIVE

"There aren't many lights up here, are there?" Clarissa said, more to herself than Toby, and reached forward with her left hand to turn the radio off. Toby had a feeling that the silence aided her concentration, so he helped her out by continuing the song she'd cut off in her prime.

"—love youoooooooooouooooouuuuuoooo. I'll—"

"Will you hush! I can't see a thing!"

"I don't get why you can see better when it's quiet," Toby said, straining against the doggy seatbelt that held him fast to the front passenger seat. He preferred to be free, but ever since Clarissa had found out—from Ed, naturally—that it was a legal requirement for dogs to be securely contained within a car, she'd taken to using the stupid belt. *Grrrrr*! "That doesn't make any sense."

"I just can," Clarissa replied testily. "Why are there no darn streetlights?"

"Because it's the countryside," Toby reminded her. "Dark skies and all that."

"Harumph."

Toby forgave her crankiness. She wasn't the world's most experienced driver and tended to either walk everywhere or take the train or bus, but she had gamely agreed to accompany him up here, so he couldn't complain.

They were cruising up in the hills surrounding the little town of Sun Valley. Up here, before you came to the village of Bushy Leaze, there were plenty of wooded areas and a smattering of civilisation with expensive houses—big ones with triple garages—hidden away behind enclosed boundaries made of high fences or brick walls, hedges and trees. The people who lived here didn't want to see or be seen, to Toby's mind.

"Anti-social," he said aloud. "Or something to hide."

"Pardon?"

"Oh, nothing." Toby placed a paw on the dashboard. "I think it's down here. Before the village starts proper."

They motored along, albeit at about fifteen miles per hour, as Toby squinted out of the window. He spotted a line of identical houses that had been built in pairs. "There!" he announced. "That one! The first of that row!"

Clarissa jammed on her brakes, a little too suddenly. Toby shot forward but was prevented from going anywhere by his seatbelt. It still gave him a jolt, though, and his breath escaped in a whoosh.

"Sorry about that," said Clarissa, and pulled on the handbrake. Reaching over, she unclipped him and took a moment to study where they were. A low wall with an open wooden gate separated the road from a pretty thatched cottage, with an open-sided porch—also thatched—flanked by a hanging lantern on one side and a side window with stained glass on the other. The garden, what Clarissa could see of it, was well kept. "Would you like me to come with you?"

"Probably best if you don't," said Toby, trying not to sound too self-important. "Apparently it's top-secret business."

"Hmmm." Clarissa didn't sound convinced.

"*Dog* business," Toby reiterated.

"Okay! Okay!" Clarissa popped open the glove box

and reached for her phone. "I'll keep myself occupied. Try not to be too long, though. I still have some work to do at home."

"Roger that!" Toby said, magicking the door lock and sliding out of the car.

Sparky was waiting for him at his front door, his tiny paws hopping around in agitation.

"Thank goodness you're here, Toby!" the little dog said. "Thank you so much for coming. I was beginning to lose hope."

"Sorry it took so long. I've had an incredibly busy" —not to mention stressful—"day, and only made it to the Twilight Barking in the nick of time."

"I'm so glad you did!" Sparky yapped. "I'm desperate for your help."

"What's happened?"

Sparky lowered his voice to a whisper. "It's my dad."

Toby experienced a frisson of anxiety, remembering the fate of Old Joe. "Is he—?"

"Oh no. No, no!" Sparky looked horrified. "Not that."

Phew. Toby relaxed.

"Worse in some ways," continued Sparky.

Toby's ears twitched. "Worse? What could be worse?"

"He's not himself. He's ... changed ..."

"Changed how?" Toby asked. "People change—"

"I know, but he's not a young man, and he's dreadfully set in his ways. I say dreadfully, but to be honest that's why I love him. He likes his routines. He likes to potter around. He keeps himself busy. He loves cooking. We love our walks together." This time when Sparky sighed, it sounded as though the whole world was sighing with him, but it was just the slightest of breezes in the trees around the house.

"And he's stopped doing that, or ...?" Toby asked.

"He's stopped doing everything!" Sparky confirmed. "He just sits in his chair and stares!"

"Hmm." Toby was no doctor, but he did have experience of living with Old Joe, who would occasionally stop what he was doing and stare into space for what would seem like a lifetime. Almost as if his batteries had run out. "You're sure he's not d—"

"No. Definitely not. I know he's not because he has this terrible cough."

"Ah!" Toby felt another rush of relief. This was nothing more than a dose of the flu! Silly Sparky! "It'll be nothing to worry about," Toby said, trying to reassure the panicky Yorkshire terrier.

Sparky shook his head. "I think it's best if you see for yourself." He swivelled quickly and pushed his nose against the front door. It swung open and Toby hurried inside after Sparky through to a cosily lit hallway, a set of wide, thickly carpeted stairs climbing away from them, and a number of pictures of Dartmoor adorning the walls. The house, although generally clean, had an aroma of spoiled food—sour milk and stinky cheese.

And boy, was it warm.

"Blimey," Toby panted, instantly overheating.

"Dad feels the cold," said Sparky.

"It's been about two hundred degrees outside today," Toby reminded him. "There's been no cold to feel!"

"He put the heating on a few days ago and hasn't turned it down since." Sparky shrugged, his ears slightly crooked. "I'm not so young myself. I don't mind it warm."

"There's *warm*, and there's dropped-into-the-centre-of-a-volcano-to-boil-alive warm—and this is definitely the latter."

"You may be right," Sparky agreed. "My water bowl dried up two days ago. I've been having to drink out of the bird bath in the garden. There's not much in it, so I've been rationing myself."

From the direction of the living room came an odd noise. Toby tilted his head to listen, then tentatively took a few steps towards the lounge. The noise came again. "Caaaooowwwwwh!"

Cow?

"Caaaooowwwwwh!"

Kind of ... throaty. Hoarse. A bit like when a vacuum cleaner hoovers up a load of dried leaves.

"You're right," Toby whispered. "That *is* a terrible cough." He jerked his head towards the front of the house. "I can ask Clarissa to call a doctor—"

"I think that might be the best thing to do." Sparky sounded reluctant. "But—"

"Caaaooowwwwwh!"

Something clunked. "Oh. I think Dad's dropped the TV remote again. One second." Sparky hurried through into the living room, out of Toby's immediate sight. "Alright, Dad?" he heard Sparky say. "Let me pick this up for you."

He followed Sparky into the living room. A pleasant space, probably last decorated—in cream and peach—twenty years previously, but smart and cosy with a comfortable three-piece suite, piles of books on the occasional tables and more paintings of wild landscapes on the walls.

'Dad' was sitting in one of the two armchairs—one of those with the lever that pushes out a footrest—with a good view of the television. There was some sort of documentary about fish on the screen, which, to Toby's quick eye, was rather like standing next to the glass in an aquarium. Sparky picked up the remote in his mouth and deposited it on the armrest.

"Caaaooowwwwwh!"

"Here you are, Dad," said Sparky.

"Brainnnnnnns," said Dad.

"Huh?" Toby pricked his ears up.

"That's all he does," said Sparky. "He says 'brains' and he coughs. He's said little else for the best part of three days."

"Mmm, that's weird," Toby said, an alarm bell tinkling in the back of his mind.

"Helloooo?" Clarissa had evidently grown impatient. Toby heard her rap on the front door. "Hello? It's Clarissa. Is everything alright?"

Sparky scampered out into the hallway to show her where they were. A moment later she stuck her head around the door. "Hello, Mr ... erm ... Sorry to intrude, but—"

"Caaaooowwwwwh!"

"Ooh. That's nasty." Clarissa came fully into the living room and approached Dad in his armchair. "Croup? Whooping cough, perhaps? We should definitely call you a doctor. Or an ambulance, perhaps."

Sparky hovered, uncertain of what to do.

"I've left my phone in the car. Is it okay if I use yours?" Clarissa asked, crouching next to Sparky's dad and reaching out to pat his arm.

As soon as she made contact, the reaction was instantaneous. Dad's head twisted ninety degrees with a loud click. "Braaainnnns!" he spat, spraying the air with his toxic breath. Toby had a nanosecond to notice Sparky's dad's oddly green colouring before the man's hand shot out like a missile, attempting to grab Clarissa by the throat.

Clarissa screamed and tumbled backwards, brushing at her neck as though the feel of Dad's fingers had repulsed her.

"Dad! Dad!" shouted Sparky. "Dad, stop!"

Dad lurched out of his seat, his limbs moving stiffly, eyes locked on Clarissa.

"Ohmydogness!" Toby lamented, unsure what to do.

"Change the channel," Sparky cried.

"What?" Toby frowned.

"Change the TV channel!"

"What to?" Toby asked. Changing channels was something he was most adept at. He didn't enjoy any of those mid-morning discussion programmes. Too much yakkity-yak. He much preferred a cooking programme or, best of all, a murder mystery!

"Football!" Sparky shouted. "Put some football on!"

Toby waved a paw at the screen and began flipping through the channels. At this time of night, there had to be something somewhere ... oh! There!

The sound of the crowd caught Sparky's dad's attention, somehow wheedling its way into his fuzzy mind. He jolted upright and turned to face the television. "Baaaallllls!" he drawled. "Offsssssssside!!"

Sparky jumped up and caught hold of Dad's shirt sleeve. "Help me," he mumbled to Toby through a mouthful of cloth. Toby hurried to the other side to guide Dad back to his armchair. Sparky's dad collapsed, mouth open, staring at the screen as twenty-two mini men ran around after a pig's bladder on the world's most perfect lawn.

"Baaallllllllsss!" he hissed once more, before lapsing into silence.

Clarissa drew in a shaky breath and scrambled backwards on her bottom until she was well clear of the man's reach. "What's his problem?" she whispered, scrambling to her feet. "That's not whooping cough—"

"I think I know what it is!" Toby announced. The cogs whirring away in Toby's brain had finally clicked into place. He'd seen this 'illness' before. On late-night television. Old Joe had often struggled with insomnia, so he would cuddle up on the sofa with Toby, wrapping them both in a big fluffy blanket and turning on a horror film. One of those films, *Night of the Living Dead*, had characters with much the same symptoms as Sparky's dad.

"He's a zombie!"

CHAPTER SIX

"What are we going to do?" Sparky whispered. He had started to pant, visibly anxious about what was happening with his dad.

"That's a good question," Toby said. They were huddled in the hall, ears twitching, listening for the slightest hint that Sparky's dad had dragged himself to his feet again and had decided to come after them.

"Maybe I should call someone." Clarissa retreated into the kitchen and fumbled around for a light switch.

"Who can you call?" Toby asked.

Clarissa blinked as the kitchen flooded with light. "I have no idea." She stared at her phone display, her mouth twisted, thinking. "I suppose I could call an ambulance."

"Do hospitals see many cases of zombies?" Toby asked.

"Probably not," Clarissa admitted. "Would they know what to do? What about the police? They have to deal with everything, don't they? From gas leaks to UFOs."

Toby cocked his head. "UFOs?" He'd have to have a word with Not-so-dead-to-me Ed about that. Intriguing!

"You know what I mean," said Clarissa.

Toby didn't, but decided to park the UFO subject. Or dock it, because wasn't that what you did with spaceships? For now.

Sparky fretted. "We can't call the police. All they do is arrest people. I don't want my dad arrested. He hasn't done anything wrong. He's just ... a bit poorly."

Toby exchanged glances with Clarissa. *A bit poorly*? The Yorkshire terrier was deluded.

"They might be able to suggest where we could take him," Clarissa said. "That's all I'm thinking. We could reach out to someone who would know how to help—"

"Although Sparky does have a point when you think about it." Toby stopped her in full flow. "I was watching a documentary about Roswell a few weeks ago—"

"Oh, Toby," Clarissa sighed. "You're not going to start spouting conspiracy theories at me, are you? You shouldn't watch such things. I'm going to have to confiscate the remote, aren't I?"

Toby yelped, appalled at the very idea. "Certainly not!" He *loved* television! How dare she! "All I'm saying is that—" He darted a quick look at Sparky and then lowered his voice, trying to talk out of the corner of his mouth. This wasn't possible because he was a dog, and dogs can't do that.

Even humans struggle.

Toby gave up trying and reverted to his usual way of speaking. "All I'm saying is that when the authorities find out about—" He floundered, trying to come up with a way to communicate what he was trying to say.

"Odd occurrences?" Sparky suggested. "Unusual events?"

"Exactly!" Toby said. "Thank you." He nodded with satisfaction at Clarissa. "When the authorities find out about certain *odd* occurrences and *unusual* events they tend to send *officials*, and then all of a sudden, the problem *disappears*."

"That's what we want." Clarissa began to key in numbers on the phone. "We *want* to rid ourselves of the problem."

"But not *permanently*!" Toby exclaimed, jerking his head towards Sparky.

"Ah." Clarissa's finger paused in mid-air. "I see what you're saying."

"What *are* you saying?" Sparky seemed confused. "You think official hoomans would come and take my dad away and I'd never see him again?" His voice rose at the end both in pitch and volume.

"Ssshhh!" Toby bared his teeth and nodded at the wall. The zombie was only on the other side. The last thing they needed was to alert the old man to what they were discussing and have him bolt. Toby had watched enough zombie films to know that he didn't want to set a zombie loose in the countryside.

"Well, do you?" Sparky demanded, but more quietly this time.

"We're not going to let that happen," Toby reassured his friend.

"Aren't we?" Clarissa muttered.

Toby heard her anyway, of course. "No, we're *not*," he said. "We have to look after Sparky's dad."

Clarissa slumped over the kitchen table and put her head in her hands. "I have a deadline, Toby. I have to finish my work. You told me this wouldn't take long."

"I didn't realise it was an emergency," Toby said.

"Sparky helped me once, so of course I want to return the favour."

"I understand, I do. It's just—"

"Look. Why don't you go home and do what you have to do, and I'll stay here tonight with Sparky to keep an eye on his dad. Then tomorrow morning we can reconvene and decide what to do next."

Clarissa removed her hands from her face and stared first at Toby and then at Sparky. "That's a plan."

"A pretty good one, I reckon." Toby wiggled his head, slightly smug.

Clarissa raised her eyebrows in Sparky's direction. "What do you think?"

"I think if I stay near my dad and maybe Toby sleeps out here in the kitchen, it would be okay. He hasn't moved much over the past few days."

Clarissa sighed deeply, biting her lip while she considered her options. Finally, she nodded. "Alright. I'll go home and work, and I'll come back first thing in the morning." She pushed her chair back, pocketing her phone. Scanning the room, she noted Sparky's empty food and water bowls. "Let me refill these," she said, and quickly searched the cupboard for some dry dog mix. She poured some into Sparky's dinner bowl, a ceramic dish decorated with bow ties. He sniffed at it and curled his lip.

"Alrighty then." Clarissa filled the water bowl and hurriedly stepped back as both dogs dived towards it.

In the interests of politeness, Toby held back. Sparky's need was greater than his—after all, he'd been stuck here alone for a few days. He watched in awe as Sparky drank the contents straight off.

Clarissa refilled the bowl. *My turn!* thought Toby, but as his lips went in for the chill, Sparky jumped in front of him and began lapping away again.

Sheesh. "Careful, mate," Toby said. "Too much water too quickly can have pee-percussions."

Clarissa topped the bowl up for the third time before hurrying off to locate the central heating controls in the hall and turn the heating off before everyone in the house melted.

Once Toby had managed to take a turn with the water, and Sparky's thirst seemed to be quenched, at least temporarily, Clarissa reached down to stroke Toby's head. "Right," she said. "Be good."

"I'm always good." *Duh!*

Toby walked her to the front door and watched her climb into her car and drive away before quietly pushing the door to.

He turned back to Sparky, standing behind him, his ears drooping, his beard wet from all the water. "I think we should take it in turns to watch over your dad tonight."

Sparky nodded, miserable. "I'd appreciate that. I'm exhausted."

"You should eat," Toby said. "That would help."

Sparky shook his head, droplets of water flying. "I'm not that hungry."

Toby couldn't imagine not being hungry. Ever. He padded into the kitchen and examined the mix in Sparky's bowl. On second thoughts, it didn't look overly appetising. Clarissa could at least have prepared them a sammich before she swanned off. He sniffed, partly in disdain and partly to see whether he could find anything interesting on the worktops, but given the heat of the house, it probably wouldn't be a good idea to eat anything that had been left out over the past few days.

"Do you want to watch the television with us?" Sparky asked.

Toby considered his options. As much as he loved television, he didn't want Sparky's dad to become agitated by his presence. "I'll take my watch in the hallway," he decided.

"Why don't I go first?" Sparky asked. "I can keep him calm for the next hour or so, and by the time you take over, he'll be sleeping like a puppy."

Toby doubted that, somehow. "Are you sure? I don't mind going first ... and you said you were tired."

"I'll be fine," Sparky assured him.

"Alright. Probably best if I go straight to bed," Toby said. "I'll grab forty winks, and you can wake me up in an hour or two."

"Roger, wilco! You can use my basket in the kitchen if you like," Sparky told him. "Just move some of my toys out of it. I'm a bit old for toys now, but Old Pete hangs onto them for sentiment's sake."

"Old Pete?" Toby liked that name. It sounded like Old Joe. He also liked the sound of toys, but he gratefully declined. "No offence," he said, "but ... er ... don't you have any beds? Like proper hooman beds with pillows and mattress and covers?"

"Well, yes," said Sparky, "but—"

"I won't make a mess," promised Toby. "I don't shed. I don't have fleas. It'll be cool."

"Oh." Sparky seemed a little taken aback. "Upstairs—"

Before the little dog could say another word, Toby bounded up the stairs two at a time and began exploring, nudging open the doors to see what he could find, like a canine Goldilocks. He located the bathroom, a towel draped over the radiator, and Sparky's dad's shaving kit neatly lined up on the windowsill. The next room turned out to be the main bedroom, with a pile of books on the bedside table and a handmade rug by the bed. Toby quickly decided against both of those options and settled instead on the bed in one of the spare rooms. Jumping up and nesting among the covers, he nestled into a tight doughnut shape. For a while, he listened, one ear perky, hearing owls outside and the distant barking of a pug who'd been let out for his evening ablutions but been forgotten about.

You need a dog flap, mate.

Toby's thoughts idled away. He wondered how Clarissa was getting on with her newspaper article. And was she missing him? From time to time, he heard the distant sound of a hacking cough, but eventually nothing could keep him awake any longer. His eyes closed and his ear relaxed ... and he left Sparky to the night's first watch.

CHAPTER SEVEN

The problem was, Sparky was old. And a bit blind. And a bit deaf.

Old dogs who are a bit blind and a bit deaf don't generally make for good watchdogs.

When the shrilling of the telephone jarred Toby from his pleasant slumber the following morning, the sun was already climbing in the sky, promising another glorious day. For a brief moment, heart thumping, Toby couldn't place where he was. The smells were as unfamiliar as the surroundings. As soon as he did remember, however, he jumped from the bed and hurried downstairs, staring at the trilling telephone on the table by the front door as he passed it.

Inching his snout into the living room, he peeked around the door, fearing that Old Pete had ripped

Sparky limb from limb. After all, only the demise of the Yorkshire terrier could properly explain why Sparky hadn't woken Toby to keep watch over the old chap ...

As Toby peered into the lounge, three things became quickly apparent. One, the television was replaying the previous day's football matches. Two, Sparky—lying on his side on the rug in front of the dormant fire and now staring back at Toby with huge sleepy boogers in the corner of his eyes—had only just woken up himself. And three, Old Pete was gone.

"Jeepers!" Toby barked. "Where is he?"

"Huh?" Sparky bolted upright, his neck cricking as he did so. "Ow!"

"Where's your dad?" Toby hurried over and jumped onto the recliner. The seat was warm, as though someone had only recently vacated it. Dropping back to the floor, nose to the carpet, Toby began sniffing around.

"Oh my!" Sparky pulled himself together and rushed out into the hallway, barking frantically. "Dad? Dad?" He paused at the foot of the staircase and barked upwards. "Are you in the bathroom, Dad? Where are you?"

Toby followed Sparky's dad's fragrant—he evidently hadn't showered or shaved or even brushed his teeth for a few days—trail all the way to the front door. "I think he's gone outside," he said.

Sparky used his nose to edge the door ajar and the two dogs hurried out into the front garden, Toby scenting as he went. A peculiar musky, meaty, unwashed zombie smell continued along the path right to the gate.

The gate stood open, even though Clarissa had closed it on her way out the previous evening.

"Oh dear," said Toby.

They stood there together, scanning left and right and straight ahead, but of Old Pete there was no sign.

Toby thought about giving Sparky a dressing down, but what good would that do? The damage was done now. "Maybe he's gone for a walk?" Toby wondered.

"Without me?" Sparky didn't like the sound of that. "He'd never do that."

A bus trundled past them, an old Devon General with a diesel engine, trailing a cloud of fumes in its wake.

"Poo! Stinky!" Sparky grumbled.

"Does your dad drive?" Toby asked. He assumed the old fella did, because most hoomans seemed to.

"He does." Sparky pointed at a shiny blue car parked a little further up the road. "That's ours."

"That's a relief," Toby said. "He can't have gone far." Although in reality, there was no way of knowing what time he'd left, except his chair had been warm ...

The bus had disappeared around the bend now, but Sparky stared thoughtfully after it. "He does have a bus pass, though."

"What's a bus pass?" Toby asked. "Something that means you always have to let a bus pass you? Or that means you have right of way, or ... ?"

"No, no. It's like a ticket," Sparky told him. "It means he can use the buses as much as he likes without paying. These days we only use the car when we need to go shopping. Most other times, we just take the bus. He has to pay for me but I'm only fifty pence."

"Bargain." Now it was Toby's turn to stare in the direction the bus had taken. If he wasn't much mistaken, and let's face it, he rarely was, the bus had been heading into town.

"I'm worth more than that, admittedly," Sparky agreed.

"Hmmm," said Toby, regarding Sparky with mounting concern. "You don't think he would ..." He nodded in the direction the bus had taken.

Sparky grimaced. "Well ... he might ..." Glancing over his shoulder, Sparky suddenly turned tail and sprinted for the house as fast as his little legs would carry him. Toby gave chase and found the Yorkshire terrier in the hallway, staring up at the coat rack. "His jacket's gone," Sparky said, nose in the air. "The light-weight one he wears in the summer in case it rains. It's navy blue."

Sparky's dad had the wherewithal to remember his jacket and, possibly, his bus pass. This gave Toby hope that all was not lost. He'd never seen a zombie film yet where the zombie had flashed a bus pass at a bus driver, or remembered to take a mack with them in case the weather suddenly turned inclement.

"Perhaps he woke up this morning and felt better," suggested Toby.

"He's taken my lead, too!" Sparky sounded more put out by this than anything else. "It must have been in his pocket!"

"Oh," said Toby. That put paid to the idea that the old fellow was completely compos mentis. Why would he take the lead but not his dog?

His ears jerked up. In the distance he heard the sound of Clarissa's car. "Aha! Not to worry!" He nudged Sparky. "I think the cavalry is arriving."

They waited for her at the gate. She regarded them curiously as she parallel parked, scraping the tyres on the kerb but hardly noticing, and hurried out of the car almost the second she pulled the handbrake on.

"What's going on?" she demanded, eyes narrowed at Toby and hands on hips. "Something must be going on. I'd recognise that innocent look on your face any day of the week!"

"Good morning to you, too, Clarissa," Toby sang. "Did you ... erm ...finish your article?"

Clarissa wagged a finger at him. "Ah-ah. Don't change the subject. Where's the patient?"

She knows me too well, Toby decided. "He's ..." He looked away, suddenly finding a flea in his armpit that required urgent extermination.

"Gone," Clarissa finished for him. "That's what you're trying to tell me, isn't it?"

"You see—" Toby tried to explain.

"I thought you were going to keep an eye on him!" Clarissa sounded properly cross. Toby half expected her to stamp a foot any moment.

"Well ..." How could he explain without dropping Sparky deep in the doo-doo? After all, Sparky had had first watch. It didn't occur to Toby that he had any responsibility in the whole debacle and should have ensured Sparky had some rest before taking any sort of watch.

"Is he still ... zombified?" Clarissa asked, her lip curled.

Toby wobbled his head. "We're not sure."

"You're not sure of much, are you, buster?" Clarissa rocked back on her heels and stared at the blue sky momentarily before returning to her questioning. "Where's he gone?"

That was easier to answer. "We have no idea."

Clarissa groaned. "I don't believe this!"

"He has a bus pass," Toby relayed to Clarissa. "We think he may have taken the bus into town. Not that long ago, either."

"Really?" The news seemed to give Clarissa hope. She opened the car door. "I passed a bus as I was coming up the hill. We'd better go and look for him then!"

Toby jumped onto the back seat and scootched over, expecting little Sparky to follow him in, but Sparky did nothing of the sort. Instead he took a step back and aligned himself with his gate.

"Sparky, come on, mate!" Toby called, but Sparky shook his head and took another step away from the car.

"Dad always told me never to jump into a car with strangers," he said.

"We're not strangers," Toby reminded him, but Sparky would not budge.

Clarissa leaned down and peered through the

open door at Toby. "What's going on? Time is of the essence, surely?"

"Sparky's feeling a little bit shy," Toby explained, and gazed over the edge of the seat towards Sparky. "Sergeant Major Sparky?"

Sparky clicked his paws together and stood a little straighter. "Sir?"

"Private Page and I will head to the target area and see if we can rendezvous with the transport carrier. We will apprehend the missing person and return him to home base forthwith." In an ideal world they would, at any rate. "Your mission is to remain here and guard this post."

The Yorkshire terrier's nose inched higher. "Sir!"

"If your dad should return, send me a message the way only dogs know how."

"Yes, sir!"

"Very good! In the meantime, Sergeant Major, try to remain awake at your command."

"Yes, sir! I will, sir!"

Toby softened his tone. "Oh, and try and eat some of that dogawful dog mix, Sparky. You have to keep your strength up."

"Yes, sir! I'll try, sir!"

"Jolly good!" Toby barked. "At ease, man."

CHAPTER EIGHT

"Why did you call me private?" Clarissa enquired.

"Just my little joke," Toby said, keeping his eyes fixed firmly on the road ahead. They were driving down the lanes towards town, not at breakneck speeds, because that wasn't Clarissa's style and there was every danger the car would shake itself to bits if she went over forty, but certainly faster than Clarissa's preference given the road conditions.

"You have an annoyingly high perception of yourself and your talents at times," Clarissa told him.

"Do I?" Toby didn't quite understand what she was suggesting. Was it annoying because he was supremely talented, or was his perception wrong?

"You do."

Before Toby could quiz her any further, Clarissa slammed the brakes on, sending Toby hurtling towards the dashboard. If it wasn't for his special seatbelt, he'd have flown through the window.

"Whoops! Sorry!" Clarissa reached out to settle him. "Okay?"

"Yowzer." Toby gave himself a good shake and settled himself back into his place.

"That's why you should be secured in the back of the car, not the front," Clarissa scolded him.

"I like the front seat," Toby argued. "I can see more from here!"

"Look at that man." Clarissa jabbed a finger towards an old man pushing a walker ahead of himself as he ambled along the side of the road, hugging the verge. There were no pavements here. "Is that him?"

"That doesn't look anything like him." Toby dismissed the idea out of hand. This old chap was far too short and hunched. The only similarity was the lightweight raincoat. What was it about old folk needing an extra layer? How come they got so cold? Toby knew beyond a shadow of a doubt that if humans had more fur, they'd never need jumpers.

Clarissa huffed. "I don't know what he looks like!"

Toby swivelled his head to stare at Clarissa in

puzzlement. "How can you not know what he looks like? You met him last night."

"I didn't *meet* him, exactly. He *attacked* me, if you recall. I was too busy trying to save my skin to notice his appearance."

"Mmm, true." Toby couldn't deny that. "But anyway. He's wearing a navy blue jacket."

"Okay." Clarissa's head swivelled, looking for other likely targets. "Any other useful descriptors?"

What did she want? A police e-fit? "I could tell you what he smells like," Toby told her.

"I'm not sure I want to know." Clarissa put her foot down, but only a little. They were still only going at thirty in a forty zone.

Toby told her anyway. "Like a kebab that's been in the gutter under a hot sun for three days."

"Ugh."

They'd arrived on the edge of town now, where there were more cars and vans making deliveries. Clarissa slowed down again.

Toby glanced over his shoulder and out of the back window. They had quite a convoy following them. Clarissa remained oblivious, however. "I'm wondering if I should head to the bus station. Would he go all the way to the bus station, do you think? Or would he get off at the high street?"

"I suppose what we need to think about is why he felt the need to come into town at all," Toby suggested. "I mean ... all the food in his house has gone off by the smell of it. Maybe he needs to buy more sammich supplies. That's what I'd do."

Clarissa nodded thoughtfully, her eyes darting left and right as she navigated the traffic while still keeping an eye out for an older man in a blue jacket. "Good thinking."

Toby braced himself as she braked hard at a zebra crossing, allowing a woman with a buggy to stroll past. "I have my moments."

"Or ..." Clarissa hummed for a moment. They were off again, the car dawdling along the busy road. Toby spotted the turning for the park up ahead.

"Or?" Toby prompted.

"Maybe he has to go to the bank?"

"To withdraw money to buy sammich supplies. Could be," Toby agreed.

"Or!" Clarissa was in full swing now.

"Or?"

"If you were feeling as rough as ... what *is* his name again?"

"Mr Sparky," Toby said with all the confidence of a supreme blagger.

"If you were feeling as rough as Mr Sparky must

be feeling ... I mean, let's face it, he sounds like he's suffering with bronchial pneumonia ... you'd either head to the hospital or the doctor, right?"

"Right," Toby replied, but now he was doubtful. For starters, he didn't know what bronchial pneumonia was so he'd have to look it up, and for finishers, he remembered Old Joe's constant lament about how difficult it was to book an appointment with his GP. But what had Old Joe resorted to when he had a wheezy chest or a sinus infection? "The chemist's!"

"Huh?" Clarissa darted a quick look his way.

"Old Joe used to go the chemist! There's one on Mayflower Lane. All the old'uns use it! It's almost as popular as the post office. They stand in the queue and talk about the war."

"*The* war? What war?" Clarissa asked. "Not the Second World War. There's hardly anyone alive today old enough to remember that one."

"I don't know." Toby shrugged. "I might have made that bit up. But I do remember Old Joe talking to some little old lady about somewhere called the Palais."

"Really? The Palais?" Clarissa snorted. "That's so sweet. Mayflower Lane, you say?" She indicated and turned right, then quickly right again. They found themselves close to the market, the pavements bustling. "Ooh! Parking space." Clarissa yanked the steering wheel hard left and sailed into a space. Behind her someone honked their horn. Clarissa ignored them and ratcheted on the handbrake. "Perfect," she said. "Let's go."

Toby found it easier to dodge people than Clarissa did and, not for the first time, he lamented the fact that he had to drag her around at the end of her lead. It would be so much more liberating for the both of them if only he could be free to go where he wanted. Nonetheless, he didn't have any choice in the matter, so he bided his time and ambled beside Clarissa as she strolled along Mayflower Lane, every now and then the pair of them moving onto the road to allow someone older, infirm or with children to use the narrow, squashed pavement.

The area around the market was the oldest part of town. Some of the buildings here dated back to the late sixteenth century, and there was both a smattering of Georgian terraced houses and a full row of Victorian terraces grouped around the marketplace, along with some Victorian warehouses down a side alley. The shops on Mayflower Lane were small and square and squished together close to the edge of the pavement, their faded striped canopies hanging over into the road, the shade providing welcome relief from the already warm sun.

Ostensibly Mayflower Lane was a traffic-free zone, but because it opened out onto the market square, there were always cars, vans and delivery trucks going up and down.

Toby could hear the pie man shouting on the market, advertising his wares. No doubt Pippin was somewhere close by him, waiting for stray crusts or dropped pie innards. Pippin was never backwards in coming forwards where food was concerned.

The pharmacy, Goober's the Chemist, stood halfway along the lane. Owned by the same family for over a hundred years, its appearance hadn't changed much in that time. The front boards of the shop were an ebony colour, with the lettering picked out in gold and silver flourishes. Inside, the floor had been tiled in speckled black and white with gold flecks that sparkled under the overhanging lights—great bulbous lamps that wouldn't have looked out of place in a nineteenth-century gin palace. The cabinets were crafted from wood and contained hundreds of little drawers, each with a brass drawer pull and a little brass insert for a label. Of course, none of the drawers held lotions, potions or pills as they would have done back in the day because now everything came ready wrapped or boxed up, but even so, Goober's was a sight to behold and much loved by the older residents of Sun Valley.

It wasn't a big shop, and for that reason, no matter what time of the day it was, you'd find a queue stretching outside as people waited patiently for their turn at the counter. The queue tended to be longer during surgery hours as patients flocked out of the nearby medical centre clutching a green prescription slip. At such times, the line would stretch along the lane past a sweet shop, a tobacconist-come-newsagent's, a shoe repairer's, a dog groomer's and, on occasion, even the dry cleaner's.

Today was one of those days, it being a Monday. Everyone is ill on a Monday, after all.

Toby, with Clarissa in tow, stepped out into the road to pass the queue. He lifted his nose, sniffing out the various scents around him. Cabbages and carrots. That would be the greengrocer on the corner. Pear drops? That would be the sweet shop, he supposed. Ooh! His head jerked up. A baby's nappy? Good heavens! Enough to bring tears to his eyes, although he would still have explored it given half the chance. Shampoo ... someone had visited the hairdresser's. The pie man. Mmmm! Heavenly! More pie. No, wait. That wasn't pie. Meaty ... but not pie.

Toby pulled up and glanced over his shoulder at Clarissa. "He's close."

"You're sure?" They were outside Goober's. Clarissa stood on tiptoes and peered above people's heads, striving to see inside the chemist's. The bustle at the door was too impenetrable.

"I'm sure." Toby pulled her. "Let me go. I'll nip inside—"

"Absolutely not." Clarissa tugged him back.

"Caaaooowwwwwh!" The somewhat muffled bark of Old Pete's cough surprised both of them.

"Oh, crikey. He *is* in the chemist's!" Clarissa whispered. "We have to grab him and take him home."

"How?" Toby asked. "What if he turns rabid again?"

"I don't know," Clarissa hissed. "But we have to try."

"Let me—"

"No! You stay here." Clarissa dropped his lead. "I'll handle this."

Toby groaned and wrinkled his nose, desperate to follow.

"Excuse me," Clarissa was saying to someone in the door of the chemist's. "I'm so sorry. Excuse me. No, I'm not pushing in, I promise. Yes. Excuse me."

Toby watched as Clarissa's toes, painted a deep

purple and encased in battered black Doctor Marten sandals, disappeared from view. He could still hear her, though.

"Excuse me. Thank you."

There was a general burble of complaint.

"Caaaooowwwwwh!"

"Grandad! There you are!" Clarissa called. "Excuse me … coming through …"

The British don't like queue jumpers, but given that most of us aren't particularly confrontational—in fact, most of us will do *anything* to avoid a scene in public—we tend to mutter under our breath rather than say anything to your face. It may be passive-aggressive, but that's how we do things.

However, there's always one exception. "Excuse me, love!" An annoyed female voice broke above the hubbub. "You can't be strongarming that gentleman—"

"No, it's fine," Clarissa replied, her voice jolly. "He's my grandfather—"

"Caaaooowwwwwh!"

"I hope he's not contagious," a man said.

Toby listened to Clarissa's fake laugh. "Haha! Not at all! Not at all! A little touch of erm … non-contagious flu, that's all!"

"Caaaooowwwwwh!"

"Poor chap. That's a terrible cough!" another

woman sympathised. "Best take him home, love. He should be in bed."

"Doesn't sound like he's long for this world!" the first man said.

"Do you mind?" Clarissa sounded suitably outraged. Toby had to admire her acting skills. "Come on, Grandad. Let's get you out of here. Excuse me. Excuse me. Coming through."

"Caaaooowwwwwh!"

Clarissa's exit from Goober's was definitely facilitated by Old Pete's hacking because she led him out faster than she'd been able to make her way inside. Gripping him by the elbow, she pulled Old Pete onto the pavement.

"Caaaooowwwwwh!"

"Phew." Clarissa angled her head away. "You could do with a shower, Mr Sparky."

"I did warn you," Toby said, peering at Old Pete. His skin had taken on a deeper greenish tinge and his eyes were circled with red. He swayed a little as the trio stood there, gathering their thoughts. "He's quieter, isn't he? A little more settled."

"Thank goodness for small mercies," Clarissa muttered.

"Maybe he's tired?" Toby queried. "He hasn't had much sleep."

"Maybe." People were staring at them—everyone in the queue and many of those walking to or from the market. Clarissa frowned. "Let's take him to the car and vamoose."

"Rightio," said Toby, and between them, Clarissa pulling and Toby shoving, they began manhandling Old Pete up the road.

He went willingly enough, just a tad unsteady on his feet. Slow but sure. Until suddenly, he pulled up. "Tea!" he bellowed.

Clarissa grimaced. "I beg your pardon?"

"Tea!"

"I think he wants a cuppa," Toby prompted.

Old Pete lurched towards the opposite side of the lane, dragging Clarissa and Toby with him. For a man of his advanced years, he was still strong.

"Whoa there, tiger!" Clarissa grappled with Old Pete's jacket.

"Tea!"

"There's a café there, Clarissa," Toby told her. It was a tiddly little store with a display of cakes in the window.

"Mr Sparky?" Clarissa pulled at Old Pete's arm. "I'll buy you a cup of tea, but you shouldn't go in there."

"Tea!"

Clarissa moved around to the front of the old man and placed both hands on his chest. Enunciating each word slowly and clearly, she told him, "You stay here. I'll go." Then, wrapping Toby's lead around Old Pete's forearm, she nodded down at Toby. "You keep him here. Don't let him follow me."

"It'll cost you," Toby said.

"What do you mean it'll cost me? What will it cost me?"

"I haven't had any breakfast yet!"

Clarissa sighed. "Nor me. I'll buy a sandwich. You can have a bit."

"Tea!" roared Old Pete.

"What flavour?" Toby asked as Clarissa began to walk away.

"The cheapest," Clarissa called back.

CHAPTER NINE

By the time they arrived back at Old Pete's home, most of the takeaway tea was all over the back seat. Toby had been sitting there with the old man, trying to keep him steady. The tea had, of course, been far too hot to drink, although Old Pete had certainly tried. It simply splashed out of the cardboard beaker and flew in all directions as Clarissa navigated the numerous potholes between the marketplace and Bushy Leaze.

She'd also made the mistake of buying a slice of Victoria sponge for Old Pete in case he was hungry, but eating appeared to be beyond him. Now, as Toby and Clarissa pulled Old Pete out of the car, clumps of cake fell to the road. *What a waste*, Toby thought, but he wasn't desperate enough to begin scrounging in the dust. There was little point when he knew Clarissa had a cheese sammich in her bag.

Yum. Cheese. His favourite.

"Dad! Dad!" Sparky shot out of the front door as soon as he heard them at the gate. He barked with joy a few times, then stopped and squinted up at his human. "What's that on my dad's face?" he asked. "Has he been eating someone?"

Toby cocked his head and scrutinised the red mess around Old Pete's mouth. "Strawberry jam," he decided. "From a slice of cake."

"Oh, okay."

"Right, gang," Clarissa announced. "I think we need to give Mr Sparky here a bath."

Sparky reared back in surprise. "I only had one last month!"

"Not you, your dad!" Clarissa told him.

"He's not called Mr Sparky, he's called Mr Sharpy!"

Clarissa quirked an eyebrow in Toby's direction. "You told me—"

"It was a guess," Toby replied, tossing his head. "You have to admit it was close!"

"Let's try and help him upstairs, okay?"

With a little scuffling and shuffling, the three of

them half pushed, half dragged Old Pete into the house and up the stairs.

"Mr Sharpy?" Clarissa spoke to him in a raised voice.

"He's not deaf," said Sparky.

Clarissa waved her hand in front of Old Pete's face. "I'm trying to get through to him. It's like the lights aren't on—"

"—but someone's at home!" Toby finished for her. "Isn't that the best description of a zombie ever?"

"I wonder how much he can hear," Clarissa mused. She clutched his upper arms and spun him around, pushing him into the bathroom. He wobbled in place when she let go and waited while she turned the shower on. "Sparky ... I don't think it would be right for me to supervise your dad showering, so why don't you do it and I'll go downstairs and make another cup of tea. Maybe we can try and encourage him into bed."

"Alright," said Sparky. "I'll do my best."

As Toby and Clarissa vacated the bathroom, they could hear Sparky pleading with his dad to take his shoes off.

"Wow," said Clarissa when they made it downstairs. "If I ever end up like that, just put me to sleep."

"Seems a little harsh," said Toby, who'd nearly

ended up euthanised after Old Joe's untimely demise and still suffered with PTKD—post-traumatic kennel disorder.

Sighing, Clarissa opened the back door. "Let's have some air in here," she said. "It stinks!" Then she reached for the kettle, filled it under the cold tap and switched it on. Pulling open cupboard doors, she wrinkled her nose. "Not a clean mug in sight. I'll have to wash up, but first, if I can find some black bin bags, I'll have a quick clear-up." Poking her head under the sink, she quickly located a roll.

Why do all hoomans store bin bags under the sink? Toby wondered. *Why don't they mix it up a bit? Make a game of it? That's what I'd do!*

Above their heads they could hear the thundering of water. Toby peered skywards. Hopefully the water was remaining in the shower tray and spiralling down the drain rather than coming crashing through the floor any minute.

"We could really do with telling someone about this," Clarissa said. "I just don't know who."

Toby knew she'd be itching to share with DC Ed.

"Mrs Crouch might know someone," Toby suggested. Clarissa and Mrs Crouch had been getting on a lot better recently. They'd had a falling out and, even though it had all been a misunderstanding, things had remained tense for a while. Toby adored her, though. She spoiled him—and his friends—with homemade dog treats, so that was good enough for him.

"I don't like to bother her, really," Clarissa said.

"Ooh!" Toby had an idea. "What about Mabel?" Mabel was a hedge witch—as in a witch who genuinely lived in a hedge—in a small village not far from Lyme Regis.

"Mabel is crackers," Clarissa reminded him.

There was no denying that, so Toby pulled a face, nearly out of ideas. "You must have some contacts at the paper," he said. From time to time he travelled with Clarissa to London. She worked for *The Celestine Times* as their correspondent for the South West, mainly Devon and Cornwall, and he knew she had more than a few odd colleagues and that she'd interviewed some even odder characters.

"Mmm. But do any of them know about zombies?" she asked. "When I'm back at home, I'll have a look in my contacts and maybe put some tentative feelers out."

Tentative feelers? Toby blinked. *Are they like tentacles? With fingers on the end instead of suckers? Interesting.*

Toby watched Clarissa clear up the kitchen. She

found a black bin liner and quickly threw away all of the food on the worktops—mainly bread, fruit and stray vegetables, some packet ham and biscuits and cheese that had been left out of the fridge, and empty cartons of juice. She checked inside the fridge, but everything stored there seemed alright, even the milk, which passed Clarissa's suspicious sniff test.

Once that had been done, she washed the dishes—including half a dozen mugs—left them to drain and wiped the counters.

Upstairs, Sparky had started barking.

"Old Pete is out of the shower," Toby informed Clarissa.

"Old Pete? Is that his *real* name?" Clarissa narrowed her eyes. "Ah-ah! Don't even bother fibbing! I'll make Mr *Sharpy* a cup of tea and then we'll see if we can help him into bed."

Toby opened his mouth to protest but decided against it, feeling for all the world like the little boy who called wolf one too many times.

Clarissa was a stickler for properly brewed tea, even when she made it in a mug instead of a teapot, so they had to wait until she was happy with it before heading upstairs. She stirred in half a dozen teaspoons of sugar even though she had no idea whether or not Old Pete took sugar in his tea. "It's good for you when you don't feel so great," she told Toby when he queried this. All the while, clumps, thumps and clangs above their head alerted them to the sound of Old Pete lumbering around upstairs. Finally, Clarissa was ready. She loaded a pretty, round tray with the mug of steaming tea, a large beaker of cold water and a packet of paracetamol that she'd found in the fruit bowl and led the way out of the kitchen and up the stairs.

Old Pete's clothes were strewn all over the landing, along with several damp towels and the contents of a bottle of shower gel, but at least the latter scented the air.

Sparky poked his head around Old Pete's bedroom door. "Sorry," said Sparky. "He's nekkid."

"Nekkid?" Clarissa repeated. "Oh dear."

"I can't persuade him that clothes are a good idea," Sparky told them.

"Probably because they aren't," Toby said. He didn't understand the appeal.

"Not to worry." Clarissa hurriedly deposited the tray on the floor and picked up one of the larger towels. "Does he have a dressing gown or anything?"

"Hanging up behind the door," Toby guessed. It was another one of those predictable hooman habits.

"That's right!" Sparky sounded surprised.

"Alright. Wish me luck." Clarissa twisted her head

a little over her right shoulder in the manner of someone trying not to look and headed for the bedroom door. "Mr Sharpy?" she called, "It's only me —" as though he knew her from Adam.

"Tea!" bellowed Old Pete.

"I've brought you tea." Clarissa sidled into the bedroom, the towel held out at arm's length. "I just need you to cover yourself—"

"Tea!"

Clarissa disappeared from view. "Mr Sharpy!" Her voice rose in annoyance. "Cover yourself with—"

"Tea!"

She'd had enough. "Cover yourself with the towel, this instant!" she growled.

Toby's eyebrows wiggled in consternation. He'd never heard Clarissa sound so cross.

"Good! Now we're going to put your robe on—"

"T—"

"No!" Clarissa reprimanded the old man. "Robe first. Then tea. Come on!"

Sparky and Toby exchanged glances, Sparky's face a mixture of bewilderment and awe. They listened to the sound of some scuffling and shuffling, but nothing that sounded as though Clarissa were being dismembered, then the door opened and she hustled out and bent over to retrieve the tray.

"Is everything alright?" Sparky whispered.

"Perfectly fine," Clarissa answered, in the same prim, clipped tone she'd been using with Old Pete. "You can come in now."

Toby followed Clarissa into the room, Sparky hot on his heels. Old Pete, wearing a flowery robe with roses on that couldn't possibly have been his because it was at least one size too small, was tucked up in bed, nestled against the pillows, his hands resting on top of the covers.

Clarissa arranged the tray beside him and popped two tablets out of their wrapper. "Here you are, Mr Sharpy," she said. "Hold out your hand."

He lifted his hand, the skin that same peculiar green-tinged hue as before. If anything, he looked even paler. Clarissa dropped the pills onto his palm and mimed putting them in her mouth. He watched her.

"Tea," he muttered.

"After the tablets," she said.

He stared at her, his eyes a black expressionless void, then something broke and he lifted his hand to his mouth and deposited the tablets inside. Clarissa handed him the water, but although he tried, he couldn't keep his hand steady enough to drink from the beaker. She helped him. He swallowed and fell back against the pillows.

"Tea," he whispered, then his eyes closed.

Clarissa folded her arms, looking pleased with herself. "Who knew that tea and paracetamol cured zombie disease!" she exclaimed. "Fancy that. I must be a genius!"

CHAPTER TEN

Four days later, Toby—in perfect froggy pose as always—lay sprawled in front of the television, a dictionary between his front paws. He'd been looking up a couple of new words—as was his wont—and while bronkial had turned out to be bronchial, so far new-moan-ee-ah was eluding him.

Clarissa, as usual, was beavering away on her laptop. She'd had a response from her editor about an article she'd written, so there were revisions to do and a little additional research, some cursing and a large glass of wine.

Old Pete and Sparky and the troubles earlier in the week seemed an age away. Clarissa and Toby had remained at the house for the following twenty-four hours apart from a little trip back to Goober's the

Chemist for more paracetamol and some cough medicine, and to the supermarket to replenish tea, bread, milk and Marmite—which Clarissa swore by as a cure-all for everything. With a little care and attention, Old Pete had started to lose the horrible green colour and by the end of the next day had been able to converse in sentences of more than one word.

Since then, Clarissa had checked on him twice a day, but so far, paws crossed, he appeared to be on the road to recovery, and Toby had been able to return his attention to his wizarding shed and his studies, although neither had progressed particularly quickly. Or not as quickly as Toby would have liked.

Much to Toby's consternation, Connor had popped around. Just like that. It seemed like a peculiarly un-British thing to do, to Toby's mind. People didn't just pop round. Not unless they were the neighbours and they'd been keeping a parcel for you. And even then, they tended to be reluctant to knock on the door. Days might pass. You'd have the parcel notification in your hot little hand—the postcard on the front doormat or the email with the tracking information—and still you wouldn't go and pick it up. Eventually, the neighbour, fed up with the rotten thing that didn't belong to them collecting dust, would drop it around. And there would be an awkward exchange of pleasantries and an audible sigh of relief when the deed was done.

Connor didn't bring a parcel. He hadn't even brought his toolkit, which might have been useful. No, He just came over to see how Clarissa was progressing with the shed.

Who even does that? Toby had wondered, but deep down he knew that Connor was testing the water with Clarissa to see whether she might be *interested* in him.

They'd had coffee in the garden, 'admiring' Toby's handiwork, although Clarissa didn't admit it had been Toby who'd painted it. He felt sorry for her because Connor simply assumed she was the one responsible for the decoration and gently teased her about it.

"It's just a first coat," she'd reiterated. "I used up everything I had. I need to buy some more paint."

"I have a loyalty card for the local DIY merchant's if you want to borrow that?" Connor had offered.

"That's kind of you," Clarissa had said. "I wouldn't like to impose."

"Do impose," Toby had said, nuzzling her leg. "Let's finish the painting!"

So, Clarissa had agreed. Connor would come back after he'd finished work for the day and take her to the local Homeland store. But that wasn't all. Ho, no! Connor had slyly suggested they could enjoy a cheeky beer in one of the local pubs on the way home …

Turn it into a date, mate? Toby had gagged in disgust.

Clarissa had nudged him with her foot, and it had all been decided.

Tonight was the night.

Clarissa had enjoyed an early tea of Heinz spaghetti hoops and cheese on toast with HP sauce. Toby had held his nose and suffered through a bowl of beef and carrot wet dog food combined with his chicken and rice mixer. Clarissa had then kindly given him her toast corners as an after-dinner treat and her plate to lick, so all in all, not too bad!

When Clarissa had slapped down the lid of her laptop, Toby had flipped over the cover of his dictionary. "Time to get ready?" he asked, and stood, arching his back and extending his neck in a good stretch before doing a perfect downward dog with added yawn and limbering shake.

"I'm going like this," Clarissa told him. "I'll just wash my hands and I'm good to go."

Toby regarded her with a certain degree of scepticism. She was wearing one of her favourite band t-shirts, a black collar with a buckle at the throat, a bunch of silver necklaces that matched her rings, a pair of frayed black cut-off shorts and pink fluffy slippers. Her hair, which didn't look like she'd brushed it all day, had been piled on her head in a scruffy updo.

To Toby she looked perfect. Cute. But not date-ready. *Interesting*.

"Okeydokey. I'll fetch your lead." Toby straightened up and headed for the hall where the coats and leads were stored.

"Er ... Toby?" Clarissa called him back. "The thing is, I think it would be better if you stayed here."

"If I ...? What?" Toby wasn't sure he'd heard her properly.

"You stay here. I won't be long." Clarissa retreated into the kitchen.

Toby hurried after her. "But you always take me with you. Everywhere!"

"That's not true." Clarissa turned the taps on and began washing her hands.

"It's mostly true," Toby said.

"*Mostly* true means something is a fib," Clarissa pointed out. "I need both hands free to look at paint samples, so I think it'll be better if you stay here—"

"I don't mind letting you off your lead," Toby argued. "You can freestyle. It'll be fine."

"I'm going by myself."

"Well, that's definitely not true," Toby grumbled. "You're going with Conman."

"His name is Connor—"

"I'm telling DC Ed!"

"If you ever want to see another tuna sandwich, you'll do nothing of the kind."

Toby caught his breath. What a low blow! To insinuate she'd withdraw his sammich privileges. "It's like that, is it?" he asked.

"Don't look at me like that, Tobes," Clarissa pleaded. "I'll literally be an hour or so."

A van pulled up outside the front of the house. Music, something kind of rappy, blasted out of the open window. Mrs Crouch would undoubtedly be thrilled.

"Ooh, he's here." Clarissa kicked off her pink slippers and jammed each foot into a black Croc. "Where's my bag?"

This was a rhetorical question if ever there was one, because Clarissa always hung her bags on the newel post at the bottom of the stairs. She flipped the strap over the top, flung it over her shoulder, blew Toby a kiss and dashed out of the front door, calling behind her, "Be good!"

And then she was gone.

Toby stared open-mouthed at the place where

she'd been. "The absolute gall!" he murmured, then picked up each of her slippers in turn and dropped them neatly by the sofa where she'd find them when she came back.

Tidying done, Toby slumped on his haunches. *Oh, woe. Oh, woe woe woe.* What was he to do, left to his own devices for hours and hours?

An imperative bark from the direction of his front gate alerted him to the fact that he had company. Pippin! It took him less than five seconds to compose himself, dash through into the kitchen, leap through his dog flap and pelt around the side of the house to meet Pippin in the garden.

"Hey!" he said, wagging his tail with unbridled enthusiasm. For a moment there, he'd imagined a life alone forever, and yet here was his favourite friend to save him from a future of solitude.

"Are you busy?" Pippin drawled. She was the most laid-back hound Toby had ever met. And one of the smartest.

"I was just reading the dictionary," Toby told her. "But it's not important."

"Dullsville," Pippin decided. "Fancy a walk?"

Toby knew he shouldn't go out on his own. Clarissa had warned him multiple times of the dangers inherent for lone dogs. And not just from the dog warden, who'd clap you in irons and deposit you in a dog pound. No, no. There were far worse places for dogs to end up that didn't bear thinking about.

But Clarissa wasn't here. She'd decided to go out without him. Now he had an opportunity to return the favour.

"Why not?" Toby said. "Where do you fancy?"

"I've a hankering to go exploring," Pippin said. "Follow me."

The sun, low on the horizon, burned a deep but bright orange as they headed into town, turning the sky bright red, pink and peach, with only the smallest and fluffiest of clouds bobbing gently along. By the time they entered the marketplace, the Twilight Barking was in full swing and Toby cocked an ear, listening to the latest news. It had been another ridiculously hot day, and there were numerous cases of burned paws and vets doing good business with their salves and ointments. Fortunately, the pavements were cooler now, and Toby and Pippin strolled along together without discomfort, sniffing for pee-mails at the corners of each street, in doorways and up gateposts and lampposts. You could tell so much about a neighbourhood if you only unleashed your sense of smell.

Closer to the market, there were odd snacks to be found on the ground and in the gutters: discarded sammich corners, cauliflower leaves, solo Brussels sprouts and children's sweets. Pippin even got lucky with a pitta and salad. Someone had eaten the kebab meat from within the shell but discarded the rest.

"Fair play, fair play," remarked Toby, only slightly jealous.

The marketplace itself was somewhat of a disappointment. The traders here were too efficient when it came to cleaning up after themselves. Even the burger van, now shuttered and dark, had swept up all the onion and sauce detritus from the immediate vicinity, and the council had emptied all the bins.

"Awwww, booooo!" said Pippin, who was partial to a burger. "Not much here. Let's go up King Street. There's sometimes a fast food van up there."

King Street led up the hill and away from the market. There were several nightclubs here that the young hoomans frequented—meaning people even younger than Clarissa—but it was still early in the evening and so they were yet to open. The fast food van was nowhere in sight.

Pippin shrugged the disappointment off. "It's too

warm to be hungry, and in any case, once the burger man opens on the market tomorrow, he may lob me a sacrificial sausage if I'm lucky. Hey!" Pippin wandered across the road to where a high fence had been constructed.

"What's this?" Toby hurried over to join her.

"There used to be a pub here," Pippin informed him. "They're pulling it down, along with a load of the buildings behind it. I think they're planning on building a new shopping centre or something. I've heard lots of people moaning about it. Especially the market traders."

"Why?" Toby asked. Surely a new shopping centre would be good for the town.

"They think it will take business away from them," Pippin replied.

"That would be a shame," Toby agreed.

"I hope the marketplace doesn't close. I'd hate to lose all my friends there."

"Especially the burger man!" Toby grinned.

"Especially him!" Pippin followed the fence along, smelling the bottom of it until she came to a gap where the boards didn't quite meet. "Hey, Toby! Let's go in here and have a sniff around!"

Toby scanned the street, aware of how dark it was

getting. The streetlights were blinking on. By rights, he should be heading home.

But there would be no-one there waiting for him because Clarissa was out with Conman.

An empty house held no allure for Toby, so he wagged his tail.

"Let's do it!"

CHAPTER ELEVEN

Toby managed to slip beneath the board easily, given that he was a small to medium-sized dog and slinky with it, but poor Pippin, a little larger, had to make like a snake and wriggle through on her belly. She didn't seem to mind too much—just gave herself a violent shake to loosen the worst of the dirt from her undercarriage.

They found themselves standing among the rubble of what had once been a pub. In the limited light available to them, Toby could make out the green tiles that must once have adorned the outside of the building. The interior had evidently been stripped prior to the bulldozing of the pub because all that remained were bricks and tiles and dust and some piles of twisted iron.

Not particularly interesting.

What *was* more interesting to the dogs was that the external fence had encircled an area roughly the size of two football pitches and the construction crew had yet to clear all the buildings from the land, meaning that half a dozen structures stood in place like an abandoned Wild West town.

One of these on the outer edge might once have been a garage with a forecourt. The petrol dispensers were long gone, but the canopy remained in place, towering above the kiosk and shop. Half a dozen enormous skips stood in the parking bays, most of them full of concrete chunks, rubble and dust.

Next door to this was a church. For as long as Toby could remember—bearing in mind he wasn't quite two yet—the church had been decommissioned, or whatever you do to churches. The doors and windows had been boarded up and graffiti had been daubed over the exterior. It wasn't an especially interesting building, and goodness knows there were plenty of alternative houses of worship in town.

Toby wandered into the centre of a clearing. Not that it was a 'clear' clearing. In fact, quite the reverse. Piles of furniture and fittings had been hauled out of the various buildings and were awaiting removal. There were a couple of church pews, some mannequins, countertops, filing cabinets ... all sorts of interesting items to sniff.

"This used to be a little square," Pippin remarked. "There was a fountain! I wonder if it's still here?" She scampered around until she located it, half buried under a stack of old chairs.

"That's right." Toby remembered now. He'd walked around here a few times with Old Joe. "Because it used to be the graveyard for the church. A long, long time ago. There were benches and some flower beds." He scanned the immediate area. No flower beds now. And, if there had ever been any grave markers, they'd been removed too.

He scrutinised the remaining building on the edge of the site. You could tell that this structure might once have been a nineteenth-century grand department store. At some stage, post-WWII, the store had been sectioned off and split into four. Each section had then been given a new façade, probably way, way, way back in the nineteen fifties. Then, a couple of them had been revamped again, forty or so years later. He recalled how Old Joe had liked to sit on a bench and share his lunchtime sammich with Toby and stare at these old units for some reason. At the time Toby had thought nothing of it, but now the later façades were gone so that previous incarnations of the stores could be seen. Some sort of modern archaeology—the scraping off of the more modern face of capitalism to reveal an older layer …

"Pa-lay-is …" Toby read. "Palay … Palais! That's the Palais, where Old Joe used to go dancing!"

"He was sprightly for his age, then." Pippin was more interested in examining a black bag full of discarded rubbish close to the fountain.

"No … I mean … he used to go there when he was a young man. Can we try and get inside to have a look?" Toby didn't waste any time waiting for a response. He scurried across the debris and made a beeline for the entrance of the Palais.

"Wha—? Oh. If you like." Pippin left the bin bag alone and hurried after Toby, joining him in front of what had once been a pair of glass doors. The glass lay shattered all around. "That bag had quite an interesting smell," she told her friend.

"We can come back to it," Toby whispered. He wasn't sure why he was whispering, but finding this piece of Old Joe's past felt kind of hallowed.

"Tread carefully," Pippin said, as Toby took a tentative couple of steps into the nightclub.

It might once have been the Palais, but since then it had operated under a number of names. Ritzies. The Pussycat Club. Electric City and, more recently,

Velvet Vibe, otherwise known as Velvet's. Toby didn't know any of this, of course. He gently made his way along what might have been a grand entrance hallway, with gold-framed posters hung on red fabric walls, not genuine velvet but something similar. Holes had been knocked through some of these walls, and parts of the ceiling and cables and plumbing had been exposed. Lampshades had been removed and bulbs smashed. The floor, a fake marble tile, had begun to peel away from whatever lay beneath. Fire doors had been ripped from their hinges to enable easy access to the main auditorium.

The dogs crept through into the cavernous space. Half a dozen stairs led down to the black dance floor, surprisingly still evident and clear of rubble. The area where they found themselves, a semi-circular raised area, had surrounded the dancefloor and housed what had probably been bars at either end. There were dozens of chairs piled high, matching the ones they'd seen outside. The woodwork in here had been painted red to match the walls, and Toby noted curtain poles in places, hanging loose and dangling from the ceilings.

"Must've been grand once," Pippin murmured.

"Yes. And packed with people." Toby stared around, then upwards, spotting a massive hole in the ceiling and the far side of the building where a wrecking ball had burst in. The sky held onto the last vestiges of daylight, but not for much longer.

"I wonder if any dogs came and danced here," Pippin said, sniffing at the low wall that bordered the dance floor. "I can't smell any."

"I ought to be getting back," Toby decided. "I'm so glad I got to see this before they pulled it down, though." He shivered, imagining a young Joe strutting his stuff on the dancefloor, pulling out moves designed to wow the ladies. "I sometimes wish everything could stay the same way forever," he said. "And then no-one would ever become old and we'd never lose the people we love."

"Mmm," Pippin grunted. Toby understood that her non-committal response stemmed from the fact that she had no-one to love and no-one who loved her, apart from Toby and their little friend Troot. She never gave in to bitterness, though. "We all have a sell-by date." She turned tail and retraced her steps through to the grand entrance.

Toby followed her, past two doors and a window with two sliding glass panels, now both smashed. The sign above the window read *Ticket Office*.

That's where Old Joe would have bought his—

"Whoa!" Pippin suddenly pulled up.

"What's the matter?" Toby had been too invested

in fantasising about a past Old Joe may or may not have experienced to pay much attention to what was happening up ahead of them.

Pippin remained in place, her muscles taut, her ears pulled up, nostrils flaring. Toby stood beside her and sniffed the air. Something ... something ... kind of familiar ... but different ...

"I thought I saw someone," Pippin said. "Out there."

"It'll be a hooman down on their luck, I expect," Toby whispered. "You see them in the marketplace and in the park, don't you?"

"All the time," Pippin agreed, relaxing again.

"Do you smell that, though?" Toby sniffed again. The scent, whatever it was, although fainter than before, still lingered.

"Burger?" Pippin asked hopefully and, taking less care than on the way in, skipped across the glass to investigate outside. Toby followed her, but slowly. He had a long walk home and didn't want to do it with a slice of glass in his paw. What would Clarissa say if he traipsed blood all over the carpet?

Pippin, unable to spot anyone loitering, had made a beeline for the black bag she'd abandoned earlier. "Hey, Toby!" she called. "Check this out. It smells awesome."

By the time Toby joined her, Pippin had split open the bag and begun spreading its contents all over the immediate vicinity.

"Burgers!" she said. "I'm sure there's burgers here."

Toby scrutinised some of the items in front of him. Khaki? Like a soldier's uniform. Who put burgers in the same bag as discarded clothes?

And was that a bone?

Toby enjoyed a bone. Which self-respecting canine didn't? He licked the exposed surface. Yep, a bone alright. Proper treasure. Misgivings instantly forgotten, he tugged at the bone to dislodge it. It took a bit of teasing because it was a fair size, and it had become tangled in something else. Pressing his paws firmly into the ground and driving his strength through his shoulders, he gave one last tug. The bone came free in a rush, sending Toby rolling backwards. Laughing, partly in delight and partly in surprise, he pounced on the bone—kind of flat and curved ...

Toby paused. He'd studied several anatomy books over the past few months, so he had an inkling that what he was seeing ...

He swallowed.

... was the bone from a pelvis.

Oblivious to Toby's sudden discombobulation,

Pippin was rolling around on the dusty ground with a long bone.

Toby clamped his teeth around the pelvis bone and pulled it further into the light so he could have a better look. He silently appraised what he was seeing, then gagged and backed away.

"Ah, Pippin?"

"Mmm?" She stopped what she was doing. Something about the tone of his voice, perhaps.

"I think we've got ourselves a problem."

"Ain't no problem a little supper won't fix," Pippin told him and resumed her gnawing.

"Stop!" Toby barked at her. "Look at this!" He nudged his flat, rounded bone.

Pippin dropped her bone and came to examine his. "What's so special about it?" she asked.

"It's a pelvis. Part of a pelvis. In fact, it's a hip bone."

"A hip bone?"

"A *hooman* hip bone."

"I'm not that fussy," said Pippin, and for one horrible second, Toby thought she might lunge for his bone and run off with it. She cocked her head instead. "You are, obviously."

"It's hooman!" Toby reiterated. "And it's not just

one bone. Look here." He teased the bone out in front of them. "It's a hip bone connected to a thigh bone!"

Pippin remained silent for a few beats, thinking. Then she brightened. "You said yourself that this place used to be part of the graveyard for the church. Maybe the construction people unearthed something they shouldn't have, and rather than rebury it, they've stuffed it into a bin bag to try and hide it!"

Toby gazed at her. Why hadn't he thought of that? That seemed the most feasible explanation, right?

"I don't think we need to worry about a chunk of corpse on a bit of waste ground that—" She stopped. Toby watched her hackles rise and bristle. Strange how seeing her do that had the same immediate effect on him.

"What's the matter?" he asked.

"There's someone here," Pippin whispered.

Slowly, Toby turned around so he could face the same direction Pippin was looking in. In the shadow of the church, something was moving around.

Except, it was an odd movement. Kind of jagged rather than fluid. A lurch. The shape momentarily disappeared into the darkness close to the crumbling edifice, then, just as Toby thought it might have been a trick of the light, stumbled back into view.

There was no mistaking it. A woman. She rocked and wobbled, careering from left to right but generally in the direction of the dogs. Locked in place, they watched her advance. Toby took in the woman's clothes. An overall or uniform of some sort. It should have been white, but it was filthy. There was writing on the chest in gold and green lettering—too far away to see.

Pippin began to bark at the woman, warning her to stay away. The woman continued onwards, hair wild, eyes like saucers, arms and fingers stretched forward, seemingly oblivious. "What the dickens is wrong with her?" Pippin, eyes wide, paused her shouting long enough to ask Toby, "Is she deaf?"

Toby grimaced, the woman practically on top of them now. It might have been his imagination, but he didn't think it was—and although it was difficult to be certain in the muted light, the woman's skin had a green tinge.

Worse than that. Toby could clearly read the label on her uniform now.

Goober's, it said. *Goober's the Chemist.*

Uh-oh.

"Run!" shouted Toby, but Pippin didn't need telling twice. They fled to the wall, diving for the hole, scrabbling to see who would make it through first.

Pippin left half the fur on her back behind, but finally they both made it through onto King Street.

Standing together under the pool of light from an overhead street lamp, Pippin shook her head. "What in the actual beetlebum was *that*?"

"That," said Toby, "was a zombie. And I tell you what. I think Clarissa and I might be in deep, deep doggie doo-doo!"

CHAPTER TWELVE

"Is that you, Toby?" Clarissa called from the living room.

Rats. Toby had been doing his best to creep in through the dog flap as quietly as possible. Although he'd seen a light on at the front of the house, he'd been hoping to slink past Clarissa unnoticed and up the stairs before she spotted him.

"Yes, yes, only me!" Toby called back, glad that the kitchen light was off.

"Where've you been?" Clarissa wanted to know. Of course she did.

Toby glanced at the ceiling, hoping a higher power might be listening. "Nowhere very interesting," he lied. "Just out and about."

"Oh, because I spoke to Moriarty earlier, and she said you'd gone off with Pippin."

Did she really? He and that tell-tale rat of a cat would be having words.

"Mmmm," he said, trying not to sound too obviously evasive. He'd watched enough episodes of *Police Interceptors* to know you stood a better chance of being exonerated if you said nothing at all. What did they call in the United States? The Fifth Mam-mend-ment or something.

"What are you doing in there?" Clarissa asked, sounding a little irritated. At least she didn't have Conman with her. Mind you, it might have been better for Toby if she had because she'd have been otherwise engaged, entertaining or something. Instead, by the sound of the dramatic music on TV, she was watching some kind of horror film.

Normally Toby loved watching horror films, especially the old Hammer films, but this evening had been horrific enough. He just wanted to go to bed and put it all behind him.

"Toby?" Clarissa called again.

"Just having a drink," said Toby, and promptly lapped up half the contents of his bowl. When he raised his head, beard dripping all over the floor, Clarissa was standing in the doorway peering in at him. He wasn't sure how much she could see because the lights in here were off and he was diagonally opposite her, shielded by the shadows and a kitchen cabinet.

"Just a bit thirsty," he said, but even he wasn't convinced.

"Shall I fill your bowl up for you again?" Clarissa asked. "I know how much you love fresh water."

"No, don't worry," Toby said. "I'm off to bed now."

"It's not a problem." Clarissa flipped the light switch and turned back to Toby. Her mouth dropped open.

"Can't you fill the bowl in the dark?" Toby asked.

"WHAT THE?!"

"It looks bad, I know—"

"Where have you *been*? What have you been *doing*?" Clarissa's voice rose several octaves. "Have you any idea what *time* it is?"

Which question should he answer first? Toby gave himself a quick once-over. He was drenched. Completely saturated. And worse than that—

"Why are you green?" Clarissa took a step away from him.

Yes, even worse than being soaked through, he was covered in pondweed. Sticky, slimy, rotting pondweed.

"I had a barf," Toby admitted. "In the pond at the park."

"Wh-wh-why? Why would you do that?" Clarissa could hardly believe what she was hearing. "And at this time of night when we're just about to go to bed!"

"I was a bit ... mucky," said Toby. Truth to tell, by mutual agreement, he and Pippin had raced to the park as soon as they'd departed King Street. Toby wasn't normally a sprinter, but the thought that he'd been gnawing on a hooman bone or even part of a zombie—*yearggh*!—had made him queasy, and he'd felt the need to immerse himself in water. The large circular pond in the park was the obvious solution. The problem was, given the lack of rain of late, the pond was thick with algae and the water was foul, full of feathers and goodness knows what else from the swans, ducks and geese who inhabited the area.

He lifted his head, defiantly meeting Clarissa's gaze. Rather this than stinking of the dead. Or the undead. Right?

"You were a bit mucky?" Poor Clarissa seemed hopelessly confused. "And you think this"—she gestured at him—"is *not* mucky?" She rubbed her forehead. "You're not normally a nitwit, Toby."

I don't normally mistake a graveyard for a butcher's, to be fair, Toby thought.

Clarissa narrowed her eyes. "What aren't you telling me?"

"What do you mean?" Toby feigned innocence. Darn Clarissa with her witchy sixth sense.

"I *know* you. You're up to something!"

"I was having an adventure, that's all," Toby told her. That much wasn't a lie.

"I've half a mind to make you sleep in your shed," Clarissa said. "You'd be warm enough in there, and I could deal with you in the morning."

Toby hung his head. Being banished to his unfinished wizard shack—it could be worse, he supposed. And it was no more than he deserved, but still ... he'd be lonely.

"But I can't bear to do that, so upstairs we go, and I'll run you a bath." She pointed out into the hallway.

"Thank you, Clarissa," Toby replied, meekly sliding past her.

"Hmmm." Clarissa sounded doubtful, then, catching a whiff of him, reared back. "Crikey, Toby! You stink to high heaven!"

CHAPTER THIRTEEN

Toby kept a low profile for the next few days. He sensed Clarissa was extra watchful of him, so he didn't go anywhere except to accompany her when she wanted a walk, and he avoided contact with Pippin —through mutual consent—and as many of the dogs in the neighbourhood as feasibly possible.

Avoiding Moriarty was less easy. She came and went at will. The boundaries of Toby's small semi-detached house and front and back gardens meant absolutely nothing to her. More than once he spotted her sitting on Mrs Crouch's fence staring at him while he was outside attending to business, surveying his empire or admiring his wizard shack, and he was forced to take cover inside, away from her knowing gaze.

He didn't want to speak to anyone about the incident from that night. He found himself thinking—stupidly—that if he didn't engage with the memory of it, it would either never have happened and would fade from his recollection, or it would all go away and he wouldn't have to deal with it.

On Saturday afternoon, when Conman showed up at the gate with his toolbox and some bits of wood, Toby couldn't even raise the energy to feel riled that Clarissa was seeing more of the charming builder than she was of poor old Not-so-dead-to-me Ed. She led him round the back and they stood and surveyed the multi-coloured wizard shack, where Toby joined them.

"Hey, buddy!" Conman knelt next to Toby to give him some fuss. Toby turned his head away but otherwise didn't protest.

"He's a bit under the weather," Clarissa explained.

Toby pricked his ears up. Who did she mean? Him or Conman?

"I've been thinking about taking him to the vet."

That answered that question. He glared at Clarissa. "Over my dead body!"

"I'd rather avoid that," she told him. "That's why I think you should go to the vet!"

"Huh?" Conman, still on his knees beside Toby, raised his eyebrows.

Clarissa skirted over her conversation with Toby. "Toby decided to take a bath in the pond in the park the other night, and he's been a bit quiet ever since."

"Probably imbibed something he shouldn't have." Conman was scratching Toby's ears. It wasn't unpleasant, so he let him. "Poor old lad."

"Less of the old, thank you," said Toby. "I've got years on you, mate."

"Filthy water," Conman continued. "I'm sure he'll be right as rain in a few days."

"Let's hope so," Clarissa agreed.

Conman stood up and pointed at the old ladder, still leaning against the side of the shed. "You said you'd like this fixed?"

"Yes, if that's possible?" Clarissa asked.

"It's quite old, isn't it?" Conman gave it a shake, then put his weight on the first rung. "Seems alright, though. I can strengthen it a bit. You want it more like a flight of stairs?"

"Yes, because Toby wants to sit on the top. We're hoping to build a platform up there and erm ... watch the stars."

Conman laughed. "That's so cute. Yeah, no problem at all. Let me see what I can do."

Toby went to lie in the shade of the other shed and watch Conman as he worked. Normally he would have supervised, but today he didn't feel much like it. Maybe Clarissa was right. There had been something in the water. Or maybe ...

Good grief, no!

He wasn't turning into a zombie, was he? Had he been infected? He lifted his snout and howled. A long, lonely sound.

Clarissa started and whirled in his direction, eyes wide. "What is it?"

"Oh!" Toby pulled himself together. "Nothing. Nothing. I'm fine."

Clarissa frowned. "I am definitely phoning the vet!"

"I'm alright!" Toby protested, but Clarissa had already disappeared inside without looking back. "Oh, brother." Toby slumped over his front paws.

"What's got into your bones?" Moriarty peered at him from the shed roof, green eyes glinting. He hadn't seen her there.

"Don't mention bones to me." Toby covered his eyes with his paws.

Moriarty sprung down next to him. "You're certainly not yourself," she purred.

"Don't say that," Toby groaned. "I don't want to be anyone else!"

Moriarty never took anything at face value. "What does that mean?" she asked, after a moment's thought.

"Don't ask."

"Oh, woe is you," Moriarty scolded. "Pathetic. You're full of don'ts and won'ts this afternoon."

Toby didn't like to be thought of as pathetic. Which magickal dog would? He sat up, lengthening his spine and tilting his furry chin up. "Look at me, Moriarty. Tell me what you see."

Moriarty's velvety brows knitted together. "You're asking me what I see?"

"I'm *seriously* asking you to describe what you see!"

"Hmpf." Moriarty took her time looking Toby up and down. "A canine of the species. Quite short. Fur is mostly grey and cream or beige tinged—"

"Beige?" Toby wasn't sure he liked the sandy colour in his coat being referred to as *beige*. Wizards were never beige.

"Yes. I suppose with hints of black and brown. Shiny nose, a little dry. Whiskers with the remains of your breakfast—"

"Hardly," said Toby.

"Trust me, they're there." She continued studying him. "Perky ears. Long tail, bit of a curl. Could do with a trim. Smells of strawberry and coconut—"

"That'll be the shampoo," Toby explained. "Does that mean you can't see any green on me?"

"Green?" Moriarty repeated. "Oh, you mean like grass?"

"No, not grass—"

Moriarty snorted. "Pondweed? I heard all about your excursion the other night."

Toby scowled. "Did you? Were you spying on me?"

"I wasn't, but a friend of mine down the road spotted you coming home from the park. She said you looked like the creature from the Black Lagoon or something. A dog-sized hairy green caterpillar. What did you do? Fall in the pond?" Moriarty cackled, having far too much fun for Toby's liking.

"I went in the pond on purpose!" Toby informed her, somewhat haughtily. He couldn't have the neighbourhood pets imagining he'd become clumsy or infirm.

"And why would you do that?" Moriarty's eyes shone.

"Because I may have eaten part of a zombie!" Toby blurted.

Moriarty blinked. "For real?"

Conman, who had been busily sawing a piece of wood into two, looked over at them.

Toby jerked his head. "Let's go hide around the back." They scampered out of Conman's view in the shade of some shrubs that grew against the fence separating Toby's house from Mrs Crouch's.

Moriarty took a breath. "Well. I wasn't expecting that," she whispered.

"Do you know what a zombie is?" Toby asked.

She shrugged. "I've seen them on hooman telly. They lumber around looking all stupid."

"That's them!"

"Where did you find one of those?"

Toby lowered his voice. "I've seen two in the past eight days or so. One of my friends? His dad turned into one—"

"Oh my goodness!"

"It's okay, Clarissa cured him."

Moriarty looked impressed. "How did she do that?"

"Analgesic and tea." Toby shrugged.

Moriarty's eyes were like saucers. "But then you saw another one?"

"That's the worst part of this. When Mr Sparky was poorly—that's my friend's dad—he went to a pharmacy. Goober's the Chemist. In town."

Moriarty nodded, but she looked blank. She'd never ventured as far as town. She had a perfectly good home across the road and didn't feel the need to wander too far.

"The second zombie I saw was on the construction site behind the market—" He grimaced.

"Go on," Moriarty urged.

"This was a lady zombie, and she was wearing a Goober's the Chemist overall."

Moriarty waited for further explanation, but when none came, she sighed. "And?"

"Don't you see?" hissed Toby. "Mr Sparky or Sharpy or whatever his name is ... He went to the chemist, and then a few days later, the lady in the chemist caught zombie disease, too!"

"Ah." The lights were beginning to blink on in Moriarty's mind. "You think that Mr Sparky-Sharpy-Whoever was ..." She tutted. "Oh, what's the word? Like cat flu?"

"Con-taj-ee-us." Toby nodded. "How else do you explain it?"

"I see what you're saying," Moriarty agreed. "But it might be a coincidence."

"It might be." Toby hadn't been able to shake off his feeling of dread. "But what if it isn't? There were so many people in Goober's that day. Loads of them. All queuing for rectal thermometer readings and worming tablets—"

"I'm not sure they're a thing for hoomans," Moriarty said.

"Any of those people might have become infected!"

"That's not good."

"And I chewed on a hip bone that was connected to a thigh bone!"

"Oh my word!" Moriarty retched.

"I could be turning into a zombie dog!"

"You don't look like a zombie dog," Moriarty reassured him.

"I might be dying nonetheless!"

Moriarty took a step away from him. "Come to that, you may be infected and yet you've dragged me behind the shed with no regard whatsoever for *my* health!"

Oops. "I'm sure you'll be fine," Toby said, not even the slightest bit sure.

"I need to go." Moriarty slipped backwards.

"Mori—"

"Bye now!" she called, and with a flick of her tail and a rustle of the shrubbery, she was up and over the fence in no time.

"Toby?" Clarissa was calling him. "Toby? Where have you disappeared to? We can see the vet if we go now!"

"Gah!" Toby grumbled. Could this day get any worse?

It turned out it could, of course. The vet's examination was thorough. Toby was poked and prodded and his inner cavities explored with a variety of instruments, his stomach palpated and his nails clipped.

And to what end? "Keep an eye on him," the vet had instructed Clarissa, and handed her a bill for a hundred pounds.

"Ouch," said Clarissa, who seemed to be in more pain than Toby after the visit. "That was a waste of time, wasn't it? He seemed to think you're in good condition."

"I told you I was okay," Toby replied, unable to meet her eye, but that was probably just as well. After the shock of having to pay for ten minutes of a vet's attention, she needed all her faculties for the drive home.

Clarissa sighed. "Are you annoyed with me about having that bath the other night? Is that what this is all about?"

"No, not at all!" said Toby, amazed that she would think that.

"I put in all the bubbles," she told him, glancing at him out of the corner of her eye as she indicated at a roundabout.

"I love the bubbles!" Toby told her.

"And do you still love me?" Clarissa asked him.

Toby pretended to consider this. "After having a glass thermometer shoved where the sun don't shine? What do you think?"

Clarissa giggled. "That'll be a no, then?"

They turned into their road, slowing down in case any stray cats, dogs or children were running around. "I might come round if you make me a sammich ..." Toby said.

"You can have half a sandwich. I should offer one to Connor too."

Toby had forgotten about Conman. He watched out of the window as they parked outside the house. The young builder was loading tools into the back of his van. He beamed when he spotted Clarissa.

"Hey!" She smiled brightly as she stepped out of the car. "How are you getting on?"

"All done!" Connor replied. "I hope you approve."

"I'm sure we will. Let me just release Toby from—"

But Toby had already extracted himself from his seatbelt and opened the door with a quick wave of the paw. He began hot-footing it around the side of the house, stepping over some of Conman's chunks of wood and scattering sawdust around as he breezed through piles of it.

He rounded the corner of the house, which gave him a good view of the garden. His wizard shack stood proud, still painted in a hundred different colours, but now with a flight of steps that led to a raised platform on the roof with a guard rail all around. Toby's heart leapt at the sight of it. Conman had also cut a circle in the wall where the porthole window would go. All Clarissa would have to do would be to make sure the glass fitted snugly and seal it properly.

"What do you think?" Clarissa asked, as she and Conman joined Toby in the garden.

"I love it!" Toby capered around in high spirits.

"Well, will you look at that?" Clarissa grumbled. "I could have saved myself a hundred quid just by staying in the garden and watching you finish Toby's shack." She reached down to try to grab a hold of Toby's collar. "Why don't you try out the steps?"

Toby, happy to oblige, made his way slowly and seriously up each step, testing it for wobbliness and weight bearing, but there were no problems. The ladder was perfectly sturdy, with slats at the back so you couldn't see the gaps—which Toby had hated—

and a handrail just to add a little more security. Whatever else Toby might think of Conman, he could certainly build things. All Toby had to do was plant something vine-y and climb-y and he'd be as happy as Larry!

Whoever Larry was.

He clambered off the ladder stairs and onto the platform and settled down. He had a good view of Mrs Crouch's bloomers on her washing line from up here, and in the near distance he could hear Vita, a black Labrador who lived at the end of the road, complaining about the postie.

"Fancy some lunch?" Clarissa asked, and when Toby turned to say, 'yes, please', he realised she was talking to Conman. Or Connor. Toby decided he'd probably have to give the builder the benefit of the doubt now. *Hmpf.*

"Thanks, Clarissa, but I have to hurry back. I promised my mum I'd fix a new curtain pole for her."

"Oh." Clarissa seemed taken aback. "Okay. Another time, then."

"Definitely." Connor picked up a couple of sawn planks and tucked them under his arm.

"How much do I owe you—"

"Don't be silly!" Connor shook his head. "It's a favour for a friend, eh?"

"Are you sure? It's so kind of you," Clarissa said, following Connor as he began walking away.

"Anytime."

Toby listened to their small talk as they drifted away and frowned. He didn't know why, but something seemed out of place to him. Why did Connor blow hot and cold with Clarissa? One minute he was charming and a bit flirty, and the next he had her at arm's length.

Putting up a curtain pole for his mum? Pull the other one.

Hoomans were complex beings. Toby didn't understand them at all. Why not just sniff each other's bums and have done with it?

Perhaps it would be worth doing due diligence on Connor, after all. It was never too late to try. He would put Connor's name and description out to his friends at the Twilight Barking tonight and see what they could ferret out.

His misgivings were probably something and nothing, but it paid to be careful.

If only he and Clarissa had been a little more careful where Mr Sparky Sharpy Zombie Man had been concerned, then Toby wouldn't be frightened of what he might be turning into!

CHAPTER FOURTEEN

"We're coming to you live from Sun Valley tonight, where an interesting local story is developing!"

At the mention of Sun Valley, Toby stopped levitating the vase on the windowsill and turned his attention to the television.

He and—theoretically at least, because she'd been working on her laptop—Clarissa had been watching the third part of a gripping detective series set on a high-rise estate in big, bad London somewhere. He'd stopped paying attention to the show once the adverts had rolled out and instead began to explore what sort of weight he could levitate. Like everything, the more you practise, the better you get. He was trying to build up his strength until he could levitate an armchair, and then he'd start work on the sofa.

The national news had morphed into the regional news, but Toby had done his best to ignore almost all of it. Clarissa—being a journalist—liked to keep an eye on the day's events, but the only part of the broadcasts that Toby enjoyed were the weather forecasts. He relished watching the cartoons as the fronts swirled around the British Isles and big yellow suns were plastered over large parts of the country.

Now the old-fashioned TV was lit up by a wide red and white banner announcing *BREAKING NEWS* as it rolled across the foot of the screen.

"Did she just say Sun Valley?" Clarissa asked.

"I think so." Toby dropped the vase, missing the window ledge by a good couple of inches. Fortunately, there was nothing in it except a couple of dead flies and some fluff. It fell harmlessly onto some cushions that Toby had, earlier in the day, manoeuvred there to lie on.

"Toby!" Clarissa chastised him.

"Soz."

"What can you tell us, Abbie?" A slim woman of indeterminate age with neat hair and a strong Plymouth accent handed over to a relative youngster on the live broadcast. *Abbie McKnight, live from King Street*, flashed up on the screen.

"Yes, that's right, Lorna. An extremely interesting local story!" Abbie began.

Toby wasn't sure what Lorna was right about exactly. Perhaps she'd got Abbie's name right.

"I'm bringing you this special report from Sun Valley tonight, which many of you will know as a quintessentially sleepy market town in East Devon. Nothing here makes the news because nothing much ever happens—"

Clarissa tutted. "Really?"

"However, over the past few days, police have been called out to a series of disturbances."

Abbie turned and indicated the tall wooden fence behind her. Toby's stomach rolled. If he wasn't much mistaken—

"Apparently, ravers have been making a nuisance of themselves on this building plot behind me." The camera panned wide so that viewers could make out part of King Street and the Wesleyan church. "Now residents have called the police out on more than one occasion, but the police have yet to make any arrests."

Abbie spoke directly into the camera, her huge microphone with a ridiculously oversized furry cover clutched in one hand and a notebook in the other.

"You may be thinking, so what? The police can't catch a cold these days."

"For Pete's sake." Clarissa groaned and sank her head into her hands. "Who is this woman? Who made her a journalist?"

"Let me hand over to one of the local residents." Abbie checked her notepad. "Bryan Coolwater. Now, Mr Coolwater—" The television panned towards a geeky-looking man with a slick of black hair and thick-rimmed glasses. "You live across the road from the building site, is that correct?"

"Yes, that's right," said Bryan.

"And you're one of the residents who has complained to the police about the noise?"

"That's right," Bryan said again. "It's noisy here at all hours of the day because of all the mechanical work they've been doing, demolishing some of the buildings and what have you—"

Abbie nodded, encouraging him to continue.

"And it has to be done even if it is a pain in the—"

"Quite," said Abbie, hurriedly stealing the microphone away from Bryan. "But now you say that the noise is equally as bad overnight."

"Yeah!" Bryan was given the microphone again. "We hear music playing all night and people shouting and dogs barking—"

Toby pricked his ears up. *Oopsie.*

"And it makes no sense." Bryan gestured around the vicinity. "Sun Valley is well blessed with night-clubs. There are three in this road as it is!" He gestured angrily up the street. "Why do people feel the need to hold free parties on wasteland and disturb the rest of us?"

"So you've called the police out, have you?" Abbie asked.

"Multiple times," Bryan said, his face creased with anger. "But when they turn up—if they turn up—they haven't managed to find anyone!"

"I'd like to bring in one of your neighbours at this juncture, if I may," said Abbie, pulling a woman into shot. The camera closed in on the new woman. She had a short blonde bob that looked like a crash helmet and too much make-up. "Now, Georgina—Georgina Filby—you live a couple of doors from Bryan and you have a theory, don't you?"

"I do, Abbie!" Georgina smiled into the camera. "I've lived here for over thirty years. This used to be a nice area with the church and graveyard and a little place to sit. There were some lovely old shops across the road too, but now the construction company has started tearing everything down so it can build an eyesore—"

Abbie stepped in again. She obviously didn't want Georgina getting all political about the contentious issue of the new shopping centre. "So what's your theory, Georgina?"

"Well, it's obvious, isn't it? The construction company has bulldozed the churchyard and disturbed the souls. What you have here is the undead."

Clarissa removed her hands from her face and watched the screen.

Toby's insides began to curl up.

"From my bedroom window I can see over the fence, and I've seen figures dancing. But not dancing like normal people dance." Georgina mimicked what she'd seen, lurching from side to side, arms up, fingers splayed.

"Why exactly do you think spirits who have been disturbed would *dance*, Georgina?" Abbie asked, and Clarissa snorted again, this time with mirth rather than derision.

"It stands to reason, doesn't it?" Georgina pointed in the direction of the Palais. "There's been a night-club there since the nineteen forties! The undead want their fun!"

Clarissa giggled.

"Thanks, Georgina!" Abbie dismissed her guests and turned back to the camera. "I wonder what our viewers will think, Lorna? To help them make up their minds, here's a little footage we shot over the top of the fence earlier."

VT rolled. A pair of white shapes could be seen lumbering around, at first indistinct, but then, almost as though they caught sight of the camera, they headed towards it.

Toby shivered as a woman with dark curly hair and dead eyes shuffled forward, her white uniform even more filthy than before, and the green logo on her chest virtually indistinct.

"What in the three wise monkeys—" Clarissa hissed.

On screen, the woman's head rolled unnaturally on her neck and the footage cut off. Abbie, caught on the hop and touching her ear as though listening to messages from her producer, brought her attention back to the camera.

"It's all quiet now and the police have just driven past us, but who knows what the night will bring. Back to you in the studio, Lorna!"

Lorna's head reappeared, filling the whole screen. She smiled. "Interesting report there from Abbie. Next tonight, we look at the theft of goods from a food bank in Axminster and how the community has rallied together—"

"Turn that off, Toby." Clarissa had started to tap frantically on her keyboard. She always had been a frantic typist, trying to splurge the words on the page as fast as humanly possible, but now she really walloped the keys.

Toby slowly reached for the remote, reluctant to switch the television off because he had a feeling he knew what was coming.

"Toby?"

No escaping it. He waved his paw over the controls and the TV switched off. Almost simultaneously, Clarissa pulled up the piece of footage they'd just watched from the news website. She watched it through, then rolled it again. And again. Finally, she clicked through frame by frame.

"Ugh!" she announced and massaged her temples. "You know, I could swear that was the woman I met in Goober's the other day. The one who told me not to manhandle Mr Sharpy."

Toby remained silent, staring at the black TV screen.

"I must be wrong ... because the reporter, if you can call her that, said ... She said it was a rave." Clarissa forced a chuckle. "The woman I saw didn't strike me as a raver. In fact, I'd go so far as to say her dancing days were over ... apart from weddings, maybe."

Clarissa slumped back in her chair. "But there was something about the way she moved ..." The cogs in Clarissa's head were working overtime. Toby could almost hear them squeaking. Any second now ...

"Ohmylife!"

There it was.

Clarissa exploded out of her chair, knocking her notebook, her mouse and half a dozen pens flying. "Is it possible that Mr Sharpy was contagious?"

"Contagious." Toby repeated the word. *That's right. That's how you say it. Contagious.*

"Oh, blimey. What have we done?"

Toby slowly turned his head to regard Clarissa. She observed the movement. They gazed at each other, saying nothing, until finally Toby had to look away.

Clarissa breathed audibly. "You knew about this, didn't you?" she whispered.

Toby couldn't deny it any longer. "The night of the pondweed," he admitted.

Clarissa lifted her shoulders. "You addle my brain sometimes. I don't know what pondweed has to do with that poor woman!" She jabbed a finger in the direction of the television.

"I went in the pond to clean myself off after touching zombie bones!"

Clarissa threw herself onto the sofa. "You need to explain, mister!" She waggled a finger at him. "And don't leave anything out."

So Toby manoeuvred himself onto the rug in front of her and took her through the events of the evening when she went out with Conman to the DIY merchant's. He explained how Pippin came around but left out the bit about scrounging for food leftovers. Clarissa would not have appreciated that. He explained how they'd found a gap beneath the fence and made their way onto the building site. He'd explored the Palais and then, when they came out again, Pippin had uncovered some bones in a black bin liner.

"Which you ate?" Clarissa grimaced.

"I had a chew," admitted Toby. "Just a little one."

"I see. And then?"

"And then this woman appeared, the one we saw on the television, and she kind of ... lurched after us."

"Is she a zombie?" Clarissa asked.

Toby nodded. "I'm pretty certain of it. And yes, her uniform did say Goober's."

Clarissa folded forward and put her head in her hands. "This is terrible. Did you see how many people were in the chemist's? How many there were in the queue?"

Toby nodded.

The table where Clarissa liked to work began to vibrate. *Zhhhhhh zhhhhhh.*

Her mobile.

"Who's calling me at this time of night?" She launched herself off the sofa and grabbed her phone as it slithered across the table.

"Rowena," she said. Her boss at *The Celestine Times*. Clarissa cleared her throat and answered. "Hey, Rowena. Everything okay?"

She listened. Toby could make out the high-pitched animated tones of a woman but not what she was saying.

"I did," Clarissa said. Then, "Erm ... No. Give me one second." She jammed the phone between her chin and her shoulder and sat down at her laptop, reaching for the mouse that was no longer where it should have been and using the touchpad instead. "Aha. Yes."

She tutted as her fingers automatically reached for the mouse again, and glared at the space it generally inhabited. Toby decided now would be a good time to try to be helpful and sneak back into Clarissa's good books, so he scouted around the floor until he found the little black mouse she loved so much. He climbed onto the seat next to her and deposited it at her side. She widened her eyes in thanks and began navigating her screens with a little more fluidity. "Got it!" she said into the phone. "Aha. Yes. Oh."

She reached for the mobile and clamped it to her left ear. "I see. Yes. Yes. Right away."

"Whoa." She slid the phone back to the table and stared at her screen, scrolling down the page.

"What's the problem?" Toby stretched his neck to afford himself a better look. Clarissa was on one of those social media sites, hastily reading through dozens of posts.

"There's someone here who watched the news this evening and identified that figure as a zombie." She laughed, sounding nervous. "His tweet has been read about one hundred thousand times so far and retweeted by twenty-one thousand, six hundred and seventy-one, no—make that seventy-two, people."

"Does that make the tweet a virus?" Toby asked.

"Does it make it viral, you mean?" Clarissa shrugged. "I don't know, but it's well on its way," she huffed. "I'm not sure that's a good thing."

She scraped her chair back. "Ironically, Rowena wants me to cover the story for *The Celestine Times*." Rowena J Gubbens was the chief editor at *The Celestine Times* and Clarissa's big boss. "She's asked me to go along to the construction site, take some photos, interview the residents ... do my job, basically."

Clarissa exhaled sharply. "What am I going to do? *We* caused this outbreak. We shouldn't have let Mr Sharpy out of our sight! We should have spoken to someone about it. Alerted the police. Anything. Doing nothing was a stupid option!"

Toby stretched a paw out, trying to offer support. "We weren't to know what would happen. You made Mr Sharpy well again—"

"But not before he ran away and like a twenty-first century Typhoid Mary made everyone else sick!"

"I think you might be exaggerating a little, Clarissa," Toby said. "We've literally seen *one* zombie."

"But there are reports of ravers. Emphasis on the S. That must mean there's more than one hanging out at the building site."

Toby considered this. What Clarissa was saying made sense when you thought about it. Mr Sparky Sharpy Watsisface had had minimal contact with the pharmacy assistant, whereas he'd probably waited in the queue for an extended period of time before they'd found him. If Mr Sparky Wotsit was contagious, then it stood to reason that several people had been infected.

And where were they all? There were plenty of empty buildings on the site. Lots of places to hide.

Toby decided not to mention this to Clarissa.

"Look on the bright side," he said instead. "Maybe, seeing as we're visiting the construction site anyway, we could take paracetamol and tea with us?"

Clarissa glared at him. "That's the stupidest idea ever!"

"Oh." Toby hung his head.

"But a terrible idea is better than no idea at all. I'll put the kettle on and make a flask."

CHAPTER FIFTEEN

With a small rucksack on her back and Toby by her side, Clarissa arrived at the construction site just after 11.15 pm. Dressed in jeans, a black t-shirt and a scruffy pair of trainers, she stood out like a sore thumb.

King Street thronged with people, mostly in their late teens and early twenties. The young women wore scanty dresses with spaghetti straps, and high heels—also with spaghetti straps—while the young men wore smart casual trousers and shirts. They were, for the most part, as Old Joe might have said, the worse for drink.

"The pubs are chucking out," Clarissa told him. "I expect they're on their way to the nightclubs."

Toby wished they'd all pop into one and leave him

and Clarissa to it, but word was evidently out. A number of young men were attempting to climb the tall fence or were standing on their mates' shoulders, trying to see over the other side. Groups of single lads pushed each other around, one coming close to tripping over Toby.

"Watch it!" Toby growled.

"Sorry mate, didn't see you there!" the young chap apologised, grinning winningly at Clarissa. "Nice dog," he said. "Is it a boy or a girl?"

Clarissa faked a smile. "Bog off!" she said, pleasantly.

The lad didn't take offence. Just clumsily stroked Toby's head and then slithered off after his friends.

Clarissa stopped to watch two young men trying to scale the fence. She began twitching nervously. "The last thing we need is people going in there and confronting a zombie!"

"Zombie!" Another young man had overheard her. He held up his arms and staggered forward. "Zombie! Zombie!"

Clarissa hurriedly moved away, taking Toby with her. They found shelter in a doorway across the road. A pair of small motorcycles zipped up King Street—a pedestrian-only road—each two up, and neither passenger wearing a helmet.

"This is chaos," grumbled Clarissa. "I can't tell who genuinely lives here and who doesn't. Plus, I need to gain entry! I can't do that while all these people are around."

"Perhaps we could create a diversion?" Toby suggested.

"Please don't!" Clarissa jerked his lead in alarm. "I know you. You'll set fire to the marketplace or—"

"Now there's an idea." Toby squinted down the road, wondering where Pippin was hiding out. Maybe she could help him.

"Absolutely not!"

Blue lights flickered in the edge of Toby's vision, and a police car turned the corner into King Street.

"Here comes trouble!" Toby said, watching as the car travelled slowly up the hill, the heads of the two uniformed occupants swivelling as they clocked the throngs of bystanders. A few seconds later, their car was followed by a second, then as these two parked up, a third blocked the road at the top.

Sun Valley's finest.

"I didn't know Sun Valley had this many police officers," Clarissa whispered. "I wonder if Ed's here." She scanned the faces as the officers jumped out of their cars and pulled on their hats. "I don't think so."

Toby sniffed the air. "I can't smell him here."

"That's a shame. I might have been able to interview him for my article."

Toby turned to gaze up at Clarissa.

"What?" she asked, a little defensively to Toby's mind. "I'm being *paid* to write an article."

"I thought we were going to try and cure the z—"

"Don't say it!" Clarissa intervened. "Not out loud."

"Nobody else can understand me," Toby reminded her.

"Move along now, folks!" A burly officer with a stab vest and lots of accoutrements attached to his belt walked towards them, shooing young people out of the way. "That's it. Keep going."

"Why even should we?" asked one young woman in a pink dress two sizes smaller than her dad would have preferred her to be wearing. "Like ... what harm are we doing?"

"Keep going, ladies." The officer wasn't in the mood to be chatty. He ushered them along.

"Oi! Don't bleedin' touch me!" the woman shrieked.

"But he didn't touch you," Toby pointed out.

"Don't get involved, Toby," Clarissa told him.

"Yeah, but—"

"Just don't."

The woman in pink stood her ground. "We're not doin' no harm!"

Why are drunk people always so loud? Toby wondered. *It's almost like their ears stop working and they can't hear themselves.*

"You're disturbing the peace, madam," the officer told her, his tone entirely professional.

"I am NOT disturbing the police!" the woman bellowed. Her friends fell about laughing.

"Not disturbing the police!" her pal hooted, almost doubled up with mirth. "Hahahaha! Oh, I need a wee!"

"Shurrup!" The pink woman flushed. "I meant peace."

"You most certainly are disturbing me, madam, so keep going, please," the police officer instructed her, a wry smile on his face. "Down the road. That's it."

The young woman succumbed to her embarrassment and allowed her friends to lead her away. The police officer observed them for a moment and turned to Clarissa. "Do you reside in this property, madam?" he asked, glancing at the house and then down at Toby.

"No, officer." Clarissa flashed her press pass. "I'm covering the breaking news story about the ... er ... ravers."

The officer nodded. "Okay. Stay clear of the fence, please."

"I will," Clarissa agreed.

If it suits us, we will, Toby thought.

A little further up King Street a scuffle had broken out. The officer hurried away. With all attention directed elsewhere, Toby took this as a sign. "Clarissa," he hissed at her. "Let's go!"

"Go where?" Clarissa wanted to know, but Toby yanked hard on the lead, nearly pulling her over, and she either had to drop it or follow him. They covered the narrow gap between the doorway they'd been sheltering in and the fence in a matter of moments, but the tricky part was following the fence to the gap without one of the officers noticing.

"I'm not sure we should do this," Clarissa whispered, pressing her back against the fence as though that might somehow make her invisible. It didn't. The street lamps gave out enough light that anyone looking their way would be able to see them clearly. Fortunately, crowds of young people were pushing and shoving around the group who were fighting, and the police—all six officers—had their work cut out. From where they lurked, Toby and Clarissa could hear the crackle of the police radios. Another few minutes and the area would be surrounded by boys and girls in blue, and they wouldn't stand a chance of getting into the building site.

"Now or never," said Toby and hurried to the gap he and Pippin had used before.

Clarissa knelt down. "You've got to be joking! I can't squeeze through that!"

"Unclip me!" Toby ordered.

Clarissa did so. "There's not much point, Tobes! I'm not going to be able to—"

"You can, look!" Toby began digging at the hole, making it a little deeper. The ground was dry and it was relatively easy to dislodge the soil, which had a sandy texture anyway.

"Per! Puh!" Clarissa spat and covered her face as she was showered in sand, mud, bits of stone, slivers of brick and tile and a host of other debris. "Ugh! Do you mind?"

"Sssh! I'm working really hard here!" Toby panted. "You're no help at all!"

"Hurry! Hurry!" Clarissa whispered, one eye on the fracas up the road. In the distance a siren was wailing.

Toby inched away and sat back on his haunches. "Phew! Try and push your backpack through."

Yanking her beast of burden from her shoulders, Clarissa did as Toby suggested. With a bit of a heave when the insides seemed to bulge and become lodged, the backpack disappeared.

"Now your turn," Toby said.

"I'm just not sure about this," Clarissa muttered, but the sirens were louder and soon King Street would be inundated. She lay on her belly and slithered like a snake beneath the fence. Getting her head and shoulders through wasn't too difficult, but she complained loudly when her chest became constricted.

"You can do it," Toby urged her. "Take a breath, let it go, and try again."

Clarissa did as he suggested. Chest through, her stomach followed, but when it came to her hips, she stuck fast.

"Nooooo!" Clarissa cried. "I'm stuck!"

"Try—"

"No amount of breathing in and out is going to help my backside slide through this gap, Toby!" she growled.

"Wriggle!" Toby ordered.

"I've wriggled!" Clarissa bellowed.

"Try again!"

"Argh! When I'm safely out of here, I'm going to kill you!"

That's nice, isn't it? Toby thought. Here he was

trying to do her a favour, and all she could do was threaten his life.

"Do something!" Clarissa snarled. "I can't face the humiliation of being found here like this!"

Toby took a breath, considering Clarissa's predicament while also studying her backside. There was nothing else for it but to give her a chomp.

"Forgive me," he said, then bit her bum.

Clarissa shrieked and jerked. The violence of the action loosened more gravel beneath her. Realising this, she shuffled forwards. Toby could hear her hands scrabbling on the other side to gain purchase. He considered having another go, but Clarissa's legs began to disappear and, when her feet followed suit, he dived through the hole himself and came up on the other side face to face with her fury.

"Hey!" He edged away from her. "You told me to do something, so I did something."

"I didn't mean bite me!"

"It worked, didn't it?" Toby couldn't help but feel a little smug.

"I'm sure there were alternatives—"

"Cwooooarrh!"

Toby pricked up his ears. Clarissa gasped. "The zombie cough," she whispered.

"They walk among us," Toby agreed.

Clarissa breathed out noisily and slid down next to the fence, using it to support her back while she fumbled in her backpack. Removing her phone, she fiddled with the settings. "I want to take some videos," she said, keeping her voice low, "but I don't want the flash on."

She tucked her notebook safely away along with the lead and took a moment to steady the flask. "I hope this thing doesn't leak. It's so old. Grandpa must have had it for years!" She'd found it in the pantry in the kitchen.

"So, are we curing zombies or are we writing an article about them?" Toby asked, regarding Clarissa's paraphernalia with an element of bafflement. "I'm confused."

"Not as confused as me," Clarissa said. "I want to try to do both, and I'm not at all sure how I'm going to do that."

She stood up, holding the phone loosely at her side. "Can you see anyone?"

"No." Toby's eyesight wasn't bad, but he relied mainly on his sense of smell and his bionic hearing. "However—"

"Cwoooooarrh!"

"They're not far away," he said, unnecessarily. "I suggest we proceed with caution."

"I second that and, erm," Clarissa giggled, sounding a little nervous, "I'll follow you."

Toby set out across the building site, much as he had earlier in the week. Not much had changed. Perhaps some of the piles of bricks and tangles of twisted iron were taller and wider than they had been, and the mountain of chairs over by the fountain had been removed, but apart from that, it all looked much as it had.

That smell, though. The one Toby now recognised as a zombie smell. The great unwashed. The meatiness of the hygienically challenged ... that scent was stronger than before. He glanced back at Clarissa. She was pulling a face and swiping at her nose, which told him that she could smell it too. It was fortunate for her that humans hadn't evolved the same level of skill as dogs when it came to scenting ...

When they reached the fountain, Clarissa paused. "Such a shame," she said. "This was so pretty in the spring and summer with all the flowers and the little grass bank in front of the church."

"Old Joe used to come here to eat his picnic lunch sometimes," Toby told her.

"Did he?" Clarissa's expression changed; her skin seemed to glow. "Ah." She stared around, as though she might see him. Of course, he wasn't there. Only the thought of him lingered here. She sighed. "Why would they build a shopping centre here? It's not as though the town needs one. There are enough empty shops as it is. All that will happen is that more businesses will move into new premises and the shops in town will stay empty. Ridiculous!"

"Maybe you should write about that for the paper, too!" said Toby.

"Maybe I will." The thought galvanised Clarissa and they set off once more.

"Watch your step," Toby warned. The light given off by the street lamps didn't reach this far, and ahead of them, the shadows gave no clues as to what lay in their path.

"Where are we going?" Clarissa whispered.

"I'm not completely sure, but I think most of what I can smell is coming from the direction of the Palais," Toby answered. "Maybe you ought to clip your lead to me so we don't become separated?"

"*Your* lead. I've put it away now," Clarissa whispered. "Just make sure you stay close where I can see you."

"Okay." Toby kept his pace slow, easily navigating the hillocks of soil and gravel, climbing over sacks of rubble and other materials, while Clarissa grunted and swore a couple of times.

"Do you think our lady from the chemist's is still here?"

"She's still here," Toby answered with certainty. He could untangle the myriad scents and he recognised hers.

"She's not alone?"

"At least one other," Toby said.

"She *must* have infected someone else, or maybe it was someone who was in the queue with Mr Sharpy," Clarissa lamented. "Good job the flask comes with two cups."

With steady progress, the Palais, with its lettering etched in stone above the entrance, loomed above them in no time. "You need to watch for all the glass in the entrance," Toby warned Clarissa.

"Wish I'd worn my boots," Clarissa said. "They'd have been better on this terrain, but it's just too warm for socks—ooh!" She reached out to steady herself as she slid on a heap of smashed glass.

"Sssh!" said Toby, pausing mid-creep as he daintily crossed the minefield of death splinters.

Clarissa halted, the glass making that strange crushing sound beneath the soles of her trainers as she waited, hardly daring to breathe. She could hear the faint sounds of music. Melodic. Guitars. A fast and steady beat. Somewhat familiar ...

"*Rock Around the Clock*?" she whispered.

It seemed somehow incongruous, the sounds of that vintage track drifting out of the dance hall beyond. More lately, in its guise as Velvet Vibes, there would have been David Guetta, Rihanna, Mark Ronson, endless dance remixes of classic tracks, rappers and trip hop and numerous others. But Bill Haley and His Comets? Who listened to them these days?

Toby nudged Clarissa's hand. "Let's go," he said.

They moved on, treading gingerly until at last they made it into the grand entrance, the ticket office to their right, the cloakroom next door to that.

"It's so dark in here," Clarissa said. She'd brought a torch but didn't want to alert anyone to their presence.

"We just need to let our eyes adjust for a minute," Toby told her. His had already adapted. That's evolution for you.

Clarissa set down her backpack. "What do you think?" she asked. "Shall I leave the flask and the paracetamol here?"

"Is there any guarantee our Goober's lady would take it?" Toby asked.

"I suppose not." Clarissa swallowed. Handling Mr Sharpy was one thing, but handling the Goober's lady and her friend—two at once—that could turn nasty.

"Let's go through to the dance floor," Toby whispered. Clarissa shouldered her backpack once more and they crept on, avoiding the loose wiring and the litter on the floor as best they could. The swell of rock and roll became louder the closer to the dance hall they ventured, and flickering light made the shadows dance.

Toby paused at the main door until Clarissa had moved alongside and crouched next to him, her hand on his head. The music was at its loudest here and yet not deafening. They stared inside the old ballroom. A vintage record player attached to a pair of equally antiquated speakers had been hooked up to provide the entertainment. Candles stuck in the top of old wine and beer bottles provided the light ...

And half a dozen couples lurched around the dance floor showing off their best zombie disco moves.

Clarissa exchanged glances with Toby. Blowing out her cheeks, she whispered, "We're going to need a bigger flask."

CHAPTER SIXTEEN

"Hey!"

Clarissa, trapped under the stupid wooden fence once more, stopped wriggling and twisted her head to get a better look at the police officer apprehending her. He shone a torch directly into her eyes.

"Do you mind?" she grumbled.

"Clarissa?" asked a familiar voice.

"Ed?" Clarissa groaned.

"What are you doing in there?"

"I'm a journalist," she reminded him. "I'm doing what journalists do."

Toby, still on the other side of the fence, wiggled his eyebrows. That wasn't strictly the truth. Yes, she'd secretly shot some footage of the zombies dancing to rock and roll, and yes, she'd told him she would come back during daylight hours to have another look, but on the other hand, she'd also popped all the paracetamol out of the packet and left her flask of tea for them to enjoy if they so wished.

It wasn't much, but it was something.

As they'd stolen quietly away, they'd discussed how they could make the twelve—at least twelve—zombies they'd seen better. Would they all respond to tea and paracetamol or had that only been true of Mr Sharpy? Would Clarissa be able to purchase wholesale quantities of paracetamol? That seemed unlikely, seeing as the law stated no-one could buy more than two packets at any one time. Thirty-two paracetamol wouldn't stretch far enough!

But it was getting late and they'd decided to head home under the fence and discuss the issue again in the morning.

Until Ed had blocked their exit, that is.

"You know that's trespass, right?" Ed asked. "I could arrest you for this!"

"Oh, shut up and pull me out," said Clarissa. "I'm stuck." She kicked her leg back, missing Toby by half an inch. "And *you* stay away from my backside!" she hollered.

"Pardon?" Ed asked.

The next moment, Clarissa slid away from Toby and popped out the other side. Toby scampered after her, navigating the gap with ease. "Hi, Ed," he said.

"You're here too, are you?" Ed asked, grabbing a hold of Toby's collar before he could scarper.

"Where else would I be?" Toby said. "Clarissa and I are a double act."

"What were you thinking?" Ed asked Clarissa, handing Toby over so she could clip his lead on. "You can't go on a building site without safety gear!" He glanced over his shoulder. "Move over this side so no-one can see you."

They darted across the road into the shadows.

"By rights—" Ed started to say.

"I know, I know, you should arrest me." Clarissa held her wrists up. "I'm ready for my handcuffs, officer!"

Toby watched as a look passed between the humans. Ed smiled. Clarissa giggled.

"You're terrible," said Ed.

"I haven't seen much of you since you helped with the shed."

"Conman keeps coming around," Toby complained.

"Connor," Clarissa reminded him.

"Huh?" Ed asked.

"Erm ... Connor, the guy we collected the shed from? He helped us put the stairs up."

"Oh, right." Ed stared down at his shiny policeman boots.

"We just need a hand painting the top coat now," Clarissa reminded him. "You know. When you have a minute."

Ed perked up at that. "Maybe this weekend?"

"Great." Clarissa grinned. "So, are you going to arrest us or what? It's getting late."

Ed glanced at Toby. "The amount of paperwork required to have you taken to the nick and to put Toby in a kennel, you know? I can't be doing with it, so you'd better scoot."

"Smashing." Clarissa took a few steps away, then reconsidered. "Ed ... have you been inside the construction site?"

"Not me, no." Ed shook his head. "I've been busy on other cases this week."

"You haven't seen the *ravers*, then?"

"No. Should I have?" He looked confused. "I've heard about them. Complaints from the residents here." He indicated the houses alongside them. "It's all anyone's talking about back at the station. But to be fair, most of these people complain about everything. They don't like the nightclubs; they don't like the noise from the market. I bet they even complained about the church back in the day and people worshipping too loud." Ed laughed. "There's so little going on in Sun Valley that one mention of ravers and all of a sudden, the local media lose their minds."

"It's something different, I suppose," Clarissa said.

Something in her voice alerted the detective's nose to trouble. "Why are you reporting on it anyway?"

"I told you. I'm a—"

"Yes, I know what you are. But *your* newspaper isn't going to be interested in a few ravers, is it? Why would that interest your ... your *readership*?"

Clarissa chuckled at the way he'd said 'your readership'. "Us devil-worshipping, baby-eating, bloodletting spellcasters, you mean?"

"Yes." Ed smiled. "That's exactly what I mean. What's going on?" He nodded towards the fence. "Something I should know about?"

"We-ell." Clarissa grimaced. "I'm not sure you'd believe me if I told you."

Ed folded his arms. "Try me."

Clarissa peered down at Toby. Toby cocked his head.

"Why are you asking him?" Ed asked.

"Because I'm wise," said Toby. "Wise in the ways of wizardliness."

"Hush," said Clarissa. "I think we should tell him."

"Ha!" Toby guffawed. "He won't believe you."

Clarissa regarded Ed seriously. "Zombies."

Ed's head jerked back. Evidently, that's not what he was expecting to hear. "Zombies?"

"Zombies," Toby repeated.

Ed chuckled. "I could have sworn he just said zombies."

"I did," said Toby.

"He did," Clarissa agreed.

"Right." Ed licked his lips. "Erm ..."

"It's a long story," Clarissa told him. "I'm happy to explain, but erm ..." She flicked her thumb back at the fence. "I need another look around in there tomorrow. With your help, that would be much easier to achieve."

"Right." Ed didn't sound too sure.

"If you were to meet us, let's say at ten-ish, and help us gain entry, I could tell you the whole story."

Ed groaned. "Couldn't we just do it over coffee or a beer somewhere?"

"No, no. You need the authentic experience."

"The authentic *zombie* experience," Toby agreed.

"Do I?"

"Yes." Clarissa trotted away, Toby, at the end of her lead, obliged to go with her.

"Hey, Ed?" he called back over his shoulder. "Don't be late!"

CHAPTER SEVENTEEN

"DC Ed Plum." Ed flashed his warrant card to a man inside a portacabin at the official entrance to the construction site. A huge sign, headed *Boyd's Construction*, hung on the nearby gate listing half a dozen dos and don'ts, the first of which instructed visitors to check in at reception.

So here they were.

"I'm investigating reports of trespassers on your site," Ed continued.

"What? Another one? We've already had your lot out this morning," the bald, heavy-set receptionist asked. He didn't sound overly bothered, though. There wasn't an awful lot happening on-site. One small digger was moving piles of twisted metal from one area to another, and a couple of young men in orange vests and bright yellow hard hats were standing around smoking, and that was about it.

"We like to be thorough," said Ed.

"Yeah. Fine. Can you just sign in here." He pushed a clipboard towards Ed. "Both of you."

Clarissa nodded.

"What's with the dog?" the bald-headed chap wanted to know.

"He's with me," said Clarissa, which wasn't actually the answer he was looking for but was accurate. Ed had suggested they leave Toby at home, but Clarissa knew that would never work. She needed Toby with her.

"He's erm .. he's a service dog," Ed said, without specifying which service.

Toby smiled up at the bald man, offering his cutest expression. "Yep. That's me. The Wizarding Service." He considered taking a bow, but Clarissa had stepped forward to sign the clipboard and he was yanked out of position.

"Right-oh. That's it." The receptionist took the clipboard from Clarissa and offered the signatures a cursory glance. "Grab yourselves a hard hat and a bib each over there." He pointed to some hooks. "Sorry, I don't have a hard hat for dogs."

"I wouldn't worry about it," Toby told him. "I've got a skull that would cut diamonds."

"It's like he's talking to me," said the receptionist. "Too cute. Schnauzer, is he?"

"After a fashion," said Clarissa.

Cheek, thought Toby.

"Can I just ask you a question?" Clarissa changed the subject.

"You just did!" The receptionist hooted.

Toby rolled his eyes.

"Ha!" said Clarissa, gamely smiling. "When you've been turning the site over, have you noticed anything odd?"

A cloud passed over the receptionist's face. "Like what?"

Clarissa shrugged. "I have no idea. Just anything that's been found that ... perhaps ... you were surprised by."

The receptionist shrugged. "I have no idea. I just sign people in and out. You'd have to talk to Mr Boyd about that."

"Boyd?" Clarissa repeated.

The receptionist indicated the sign. *Boyd's Construction*. "Travis Boyd. The owner. What happens here is his business. I used to work as a builder for him, but I lost my leg in an accident so I operate the reception now. And that's it. Everything else is way above my pay grade and of no interest to me whatsoever."

Clarissa nodded. "I know what you mean. I have the same problem." She elbowed Ed.

"Right." The receptionist nodded. "Anyway, why the interest in what's been dug up? I thought you were here to look into the ravers?"

"Oh, we are!" Clarissa reassured him.

"Have you seen anyone that might have passed as a raver?" Ed asked.

"Twenty-four-hour party people?" The receptionist curled his lip. "The Great Unwashed. Nah. They're all bogging off home at six am when decent people like me have to wake up and go to work. What a life, eh?"

"Don't I know it," said Ed.

Taking their leave, Ed and Clarissa grabbed a fluorescent bib and donned a hard hat each. As an extra measure, Clarissa doubled up the smallest bib she could find and wrapped it around Toby. "With this on, I won't lose you," she said.

As if he'd ever leave her!

They walked in the direction of the fountain. Toby could feel the eyes of the few other workers on the site focusing on them, but they had to be used to the police wandering around by now.

"Where are we going?" Ed asked.

"To the Palais!" Clarissa pointed at the once grand façade.

"Blimey. I remember this place when it was Velvets. Used to come here with my mates when I was seventeen or eighteen. Not strictly legal."

"And you a copper!" Clarissa mocked him. "And so long ago!"

"It feels like it." Ed paused and stared up at the building. "It had an enormous black frontage with a neon sign. Velvet Vibes. I remember being so excited to finally be old enough to get in!"

"Did it live up to expectations?" Clarissa asked.

"Kind of. It had these cheap velvet drapes everywhere and covered sofas with cushions. It had total chill-out vibes, but that doesn't work well in a small-town nightclub where half the population of young people are off their heads on booze and want to jump around like lunatics and work the testosterone out of their system, and the other half are young women who can't hold their alcopops."

Clarissa laughed. "Sounds like hell."

Ed smiled, affection shining in his eyes. "It was fun for a while. The dance floor was always sticky. They sold drinks in plastic cups. The plumbing and the building itself were way past their sell-by date. Cracks in the walls, you know. It had a good innings. I'm not surprised it fell into disuse." He crooked his head to one side, taking in the entrance. "Are we going in?"

"Yes." Clarissa had worn her thick-soled Doctor Martens today. With socks. "Mind the glass."

"What about Toby?" Ed didn't think twice. He leaned over and, much to Toby's surprise and consternation, scooped him up.

"Excuse me!" Toby yelped, but Ed held him firmly so he couldn't squirm. Toby, realising that he quite liked the proximity of Ed's hug, relaxed into it.

"Good boy," said Ed, manoeuvring carefully over the debris field and shielding Toby from the sharp edges on the front doors. When the coast was clear, he placed Toby on the ground.

Toby gave himself a good shake. "If only he knew how many times I've been in here," he said to Clarissa. "It's me who should be carrying him." He considered trying to levitate Ed.

"Don't," warned Clarissa.

Rats. Toby sniffed, then began leading the way.

Ed was in no rush though. He took his time, touching the walls, peering into the ticket office and then opening the door to the cloakroom. A number of coats and jackets hung limply from pegs, covered in dust and faded by time.

Together, they walked to the entrance of the dance hall itself. Clarissa spotted her flask on a round table just inside the door. The tea had been drunk, the cups left neatly alongside. The paracetamol had gone too.

Ed moved further inside, reaching for a bottle on one of the other tables. "Someone's had a candle in here."

"Great work, detective," said Toby. "What gave that away? The way the *candle* wax has melted down the sides?"

"Is this where people have been partying?"

"Not people as such," Clarissa reminded him. "Zombies."

"Of course." Ed couldn't hide his sarcasm. "How could I forget?"

"Although, they're still people underneath. Or at least Mr Sharpy was. Is. I hope he still is. I haven't checked on him today."

"You've lost me," said Ed, turning away. "Hey! Is that a record player there?" He hurried over to it. "Wow! I haven't seen one of these things for years!" Sorting through the records stacked alongside it, he counted them off. "*Now That's What I Call Rock 'N' Roll*. The Beatles, *Help*! Crikey! That must be worth a bit. The Rolling Stones. Little Richard. There are some classics here."

He surveyed the dance hall, taking in the hole in the far wall and ceiling. "What sort of idiot comes here to party, though? The place could collapse at any minute. And who are they—how *old* are they?—that they're playing all this old stuff?"

"That's what we're trying to tell you!" said Clarissa. "Zombies."

"But why would *zombies* listen to such vintage music?" The way Ed said the word zombies suggested he clearly didn't believe what Clarissa was trying to tell him.

"Because they're vintage themselves!" Clarissa suggested. "They're old people."

"Old people zombies?"

"Show me where it says that zombies can only be young people," Toby demanded.

"Look at this." Ed held up a battered Glen Miller album. "I mean, I appreciate this is a re-release from maybe the sixties or seventies, but is there *anyone* alive who still listens to this stuff?"

"Maybe when you turn into a zombie you prefer older music, I don't know." Clarissa shrugged. "Maybe it's all they could find."

"Even the record player is vintage." Ed peered

more closely at it. "Must have been a nice one back in the day. I wonder if they found it in one of the flats around here."

Clarissa ran a finger over the turntable. "You have to admit, this isn't the record collection of a 'raver'."

Ed straightened up. "I can't disagree with that."

"And I have footage." Clarissa reached into her backpack and extracted her camera. She'd spent good money on a decent digital camera because part of being a solo reporter out in the sticks meant taking her own photos or video footage. "Here." Ed came to stand next to her. She set the film up and let it play.

He watched it through without saying anything. Then had her rewind it and watched it again. The zombies she'd recorded the previous night, each paired up, dancing in a strange lurching motion. Their clothes soiled, their skin pale and tinged green, their hair matted. One or two were missing shoes. They were a variety of shapes and sizes, but none of them were young. The woman from Goober's the Chemist in her distinctive white uniform had found some sort of flowery headdress. Wobbling about on top of her head as she moved, it gave her the appearance of a long-dead Carmen Miranda.

Ed hit pause the pause button. He could clearly see the time stamp in the corner. He stared at the dance floor and then back at the film. "In here? Last night?"

"Yes."

He spun around, suddenly freaked out. "Where are they now?"

"I don't know," Clarissa admitted, "but neither Toby nor I have looked that closely, I must confess."

Ed swallowed. "Are they dangerous?"

"I don't think so ..."

"You don't *think* so?" Ed reached for the Glen Miller record as though he would use that as a weapon, perhaps as some sort of frisbee to decapitate zombie heads.

Clarissa quickly tried to explain about Mr Sharpy, but Ed had to slow her down. He stopped and started her as she explained. "He wasn't dangerous. Not really," she finished.

"I'm sorry," Ed said. "Let's go back a sec. You're saying that you found Mr Sharpy as a zombie because his dog is Toby's friend?"

"That's right," said Toby.

"Yes," said Clarissa.

"So ... What? This dog phoned Toby to tell him?"

Clarissa sighed. "Does it matter?"

Toby rolled his eyes. "Yeah, Ed. Let's stick to permanent facts."

"It's *pertinent*," Clarissa corrected him.

Ed frowned. "Okay, if we're being pertinent, you knew Mr Sharpy was a zombie because ...?"

"Because he walked like one, talked like one and used the phrase 'brains'." Clarissa was trying her best to be patient.

"He actually said brains?"

"Braaaiiiiiiiinnnns!" Toby mimicked. "And baaaaaaaaallls!"

"Only at the beginning," Clarissa conceded. "He must have known he wasn't well because he jumped on the bus and brought himself into town and went to the pharmacy. We caught up with him there and returned him home—"

"Did it not occur to you that you should have phoned the police?"

"What for?" Toby asked, settling onto the dusty ground with a yawn. "You'd have stood around and chatted about it for hours. Life's too short!"

"It did occur to us, but ... erm, we decided to handle it ourselves," Clarissa translated.

"And how exactly did you handle it?" Ed raised his eyebrows. "Tucked him into bed with a headache tablet?"

"Well, now that you mention it, yes. That's exactly what we did."

Ed tipped his head back and laughed but, when Clarissa didn't join in, his hilarity faded. "You are kidding?"

"Nope." Clarissa smiled. "You see, Mr Sharpy instinctively understood that what he needed was a cup of tea. I gave him a paracetamol and he went to sleep. He hadn't slept for days. He was exhausted."

Ed straightened the pile of records. "And just like that everything was alright with the world."

"If only life were that simple, eh, Ed?" Toby asked from his place on the floor.

"He didn't feel better overnight, but he certainly *started* to. He's a work in progress."

"A work in progress." Ed harrumphed. Turning away from Clarissa, he walked down the few steps that led to the dance floor. His shoes squeaked as he explored the area. "The floor's still as sticky as it ever was," he remarked, plucking another bottle from the small stage area and examining the candle residue.

Toby remained where he was. Ed wouldn't find anything useful. Toby had already sniffed in every nook and cranny.

"What's the link between Mr Sharpy and these vintage dancing zombies?" Ed asked, finally heading back to where Toby and Clarissa were waiting for him.

Clarissa grimaced at Toby. This was the part of the

story she was most ashamed of. "Erm ..." She rewound the video on her phone until she found the image she was looking for. "This woman in the white uniform. You see her?"

"Yes?"

"That's a Goober's the Chemist uniform."

"Mmm?"

"She was working on the day that Mr Sharpy went in there."

Ed reeled backwards. "She had contact with him?"

"Yes."

"Direct physical contact?"

"Not as far as I know."

"Just ..." Ed struggled for the words. "Just in the general vicinity?"

Clarissa scrunched her face up. "Yes."

"This zombie-ism thing is ... contagious?"

"It certainly looks that way."

"It's an airborne disease?"

"Mmm."

Ed's eyes widened in horror. "And you brought us *here*?" He raised his hands. "I've been touching everything!"

"Don't panic, Ed," Toby butted in, although he still hadn't moved from position. "Not only have we partied with Mr Sharpy, but I also ate what might have been a zombie bone! Do *we* look like zombies?"

"Exactly," Clarissa responded to Toby, but Ed thought she was agreeing with him.

He shrieked.

"Ed!" Clarissa reached for his flailing hands. "Calm down. I don't know why it seems to have spread among some people and not others, but I had extremely close contact with Mr Sharpy and I'm perfectly fine!"

"Maybe that's because you're ... like you are!"

"A witch, you mean?" Clarissa clarified.

"Maybe it only affects ordinary people."

"I *am* an ordinary person, I just happen to be a witch. An ordinary, not particularly *talented* witch. I'm as human as you are!" She sounded cross now.

"Uh-oh, DC Ed," said Toby. "Time to simmer down and macho up."

Perhaps the message reached him, because Ed suddenly calmed himself. "Sorry. Of course you are." He took a deep breath. "I know you're completely human. I apologise." Taking a moment to think, he eventually asked, "How do we find them all? These zombies? If they *are* contagious, we'll need to isolate them before they infect other people. Oh my goodness." He massaged his forehead. "How do I explain any of this to my superiors?"

"I don't know," Clarissa said. "I doubt very much they'll believe you. But you have to try to encourage them to take it seriously."

"Urgh." Ed's shoulders slumped. "You'll have to forward me that footage from your camera."

"I will do."

Ed nodded, staring at the floor and pinching his chin between finger and thumb. He looked thoroughly woebegone. Eventually he groaned and straightened up. "So, while I do that, what are you two going to be doing?"

Clarissa pulled out her notebook. "I'm going to do a bit of research into the lady from Goober's today. That's my starting point. If I can find out more about her, then maybe that will help to answer some other questions."

"Like why they all want to dance at the Palais," Toby said.

"Like why some people become infected and some don't?" Ed suggested.

"Mmm." Clarissa nodded. "All of that. But also, where did this zombie disease originate in the first place?"

CHAPTER EIGHTEEN

"Mrs Farland?" Clarissa tapped on the front door again. It hadn't been properly shut, and every rap of the knuckles pushed it slightly inward. This time, the movement released a smell that made Clarissa's eyes tear up. "Ooh!"

"Meaty," Toby agreed, trying to insert his snout in the gap between the door and the frame. Clarissa held him back, however.

They'd headed directly for Goober's the Chemist straight after leaving Boyd's construction site. The bald receptionist had watched them go, his face twisted with distrust. Clarissa had considered trying to ask him some more questions, but his expression told her that would be a waste of time.

Unfortunately, turning up at Goober's had been useless too.

The chemist's had been closed.

Although the market bustled as it normally did, Mayflower Lane had seemed oddly quiet and, when Toby and Clarissa approached the shop with its black boards and gold lettering, they'd noticed straight away that the external canopy used as a sun shade by shops on that side of the street had been rolled up and stored away. That was unusual enough.

But there was also a sign on the door.

"Closed due to illness," Toby read.

"Oh dear," said Clarissa.

"You alright, love?" an older woman, pulling a shopping trolley and just passing by, had stopped to ask.

Clarissa indicated the sign on the door.

"That's unusual, isn't it?" the woman had said. "There is another chemist on the main road, though."

"Of course. No, it's just I wanted to catch up with someone."

The woman had parked her trolley upright, leaning on the handle. "They've gone down like flies in there, with flu or some such. First it was Debbie, then one by one the rest of them. I think it's only the pharmacist, Mrs Goober the Younger, who's not fallen ill!"

"Is that right?" Clarissa had asked, her spider-reporter senses tingling. If Debbie was the first to fall, then it seemed likely she was the woman they were looking for. "It was Debbie I wanted to speak to, actually. Do you know where I can find her? I'll take her some flowers."

"Aw, bless you. Funnily enough, Debbie lives upstairs from me at Parkview Rise."

"Oh, is she still there?" Clarissa had bluffed, waving her hand in an 'oh, fancy' gesture. "I thought she'd moved."

"No, been living there since she got divorced."

"That's right," Clarissa had replied, with the air of a complete know-it-all. "Did she revert to her maiden name? She was threatening to."

"No, no. She stuck with Farland."

"Really?" Clarissa eyes had widened. "That surprises me. Anyway, I'll drop by with some Lemsip and some flowers."

"That's lovely of you." The woman had straightened up, tipped her trolley and prepared to walk on towards the market. "Give her my best. Say Dorothy was asking after her."

"I will do, Dorothy, thanks!"

Clarissa had smiled as the woman moved on, then

as if remembering something, called after her. "Oh, Dorothy, sorry! What number was it again?"

"Number three, love! Directly above me!"

"Genius," Toby had muttered.

For appearance's sake, Clarissa had picked up a bunch of flowers from the corner shop near the park. Made up of yellow marigolds, they were wilting, badly in need of water. In fact, they didn't look as though they'd make it through the day without all the petals falling off but, given that they'd been half price, Clarissa hadn't been that bothered.

Last of the big spenders, thought Toby.

She'd also bought some more paracetamol, a tin of tomato soup, a pint of milk and a sandwich with a yellow sticker on that suggested the sandwich needed eating. Imminently. Toby had pricked his ears up at that, but unfortunately Clarissa had bought it in case Debbie Farland required sustenance.

Parkview Rise was rather a grand name for a diminutive block of flats. A relatively recent build, there were two dwellings on each floor and a total of four floors. That was it. The lobby, painted a fetching shade of mucky beige, housed eight post boxes and a fire extinguisher, but the floors were clean and surfaces dust-free.

For a moment, as they hovered outside Debbie's front door, the stench suggested Debbie was beyond the need for provisions, but from somewhere they heard the plaintive sound of a zombie cough.

"Cwooooooooooooar!"

"She's in there," Clarissa whispered.

Toby lifted his nose and sniffed again. "Alone."

"Do we risk it?"

"Risk it for a biscuit," said Toby. "Or a sammich."

"You're not having the sandwich," said Clarissa, pushing the door open a little wider.

Toby stepped over the threshold. "What flavour is it?"

"Cheese salad."

"Ewww, salad. Wasn't there anything else?"

"I wasn't about to pay four quid for two pieces of bread and a tablespoon of tuna mayo," Clarissa hissed, sliding in after him. "What am I even saying? You're not having this sandwich."

Toby wagged his tail in a we'll-see-about-that-won't-we kind of way. "Through here," he said, guiding Clarissa towards the kitchen.

Clarissa peered around the door. Debbie, slumped at the table, stared disconsolately back at her, drool spilling from the corner of her mouth, her face waxy white with a green tinge, her dark hair—dyed—matted with dust. She still had her Carmen Miranda headdress and her soiled uniform on, as well as a pair of well-laddered tights and one flat leather pump on her left foot.

"Hi, Debbie!" Clarissa said, her voice bright. "How are you feeling?"

"Aaarrrrk," rasped Debbie, with a voice that sounded like she'd breathed in the dusty rubble of half of Boyd's building site.

"A bit rough, eh?" Clarissa took a step closer. Debbie didn't react other than to jerk and twitch as though she was on the receiving end of an electric shock.

Clarissa surveyed the kitchen. Filthy. Dishes and mugs everywhere. Cupboard doors were open, and Debbie had evidently been rummaging around searching for something to eat. Food had been spilled on the surfaces and the floor. The fridge door stood open, a cavern of nothingness.

"I brought you some flowers." Clarissa deposited the flowers on the table and placed her backpack on the floor, in a relatively clean spot. She emptied out the items she'd bought in the corner shop. "I'm not a doctor, but I'm going to try and make you feel better," she said.

"She made Mr Sparky Sharpy Watsisface better," Toby said, coming to sit beside Debbie. "So you're in good paws."

Debbie's head twisted. She stared at Toby with lifeless eyes, her knees and arms jerking in sharp movements.

"Please don't eat me," he said. "I'm not even two yet."

"She's not going to eat you," said Clarissa, filling the kettle at the sink. "Let's make some tea. While I'm doing the washing-up, why don't you help pick up some of the rubbish from the floor?"

Toby did as she asked, collecting together empty cartons and plastic outers and piling them by the pedal bin. He also gathered up a bunch of battered tins that Debbie had evidently been trying—and failing—to open. Beans, spaghetti, lentils, corned beef and peaches. They made for quite a colourful display once Toby had finished arranging them into a pyramid.

As Clarissa stirred the tea she sang a little song, the spoon keeping time against the ceramic of the mug she'd chosen for Debbie.

"What is that?" Toby asked.

"What?" Clarissa glanced up, noticed the pyramid of tins and shook her head slightly. "What is what?"

"What is that song you're singing?" He'd heard her sing it before, whenever she had a cold, or even after she'd broken her leg and had been laid up for a while. It was something she sang while stirring liquid: tea, coffee, chocolate, soup, even the barf at times. It had a comforting sound to it, pitched low and whispery, almost like a lullaby.

"Oh, it's something my mum used to sing to me when I was a little girl and I needed comforting."

"It's nice," Toby agreed. "It seems to calm Debbie down."

Clarissa turned to regard Debbie thoughtfully. The twitching and jerking had subsided somewhat. "She likes music, doesn't she?" There was a radio on the counter. Clarissa wiped it down with the washing-up cloth she'd been using and switched it on. The dulcet tones of Hall and Oates sang about someone called Sarah who needed warming up.

"Aaarrrrk!" Debbie rasped, but her shoulders rocked backwards and forwards almost rhythmically, so she appeared to appreciate the music.

"I wonder if the zombies have been making a beeline for the Palais because it soothes them?" Clarissa wondered. Placing the tea in front of Debbie,

Clarissa dried a plate and arranged the cheese salad sandwich on it. The bread was a little limp, and the lettuce even more so. Toby decided that he'd probably had a near miss with that. Through a mixture of stern coaxing and pleading, Clarissa managed to entice Debbie to drink all the tea and eat half the sandwich. She even downed a couple of paracetamol tablets at Clarissa's request.

With Debbie being so placid, it seemed like a good time to relieve her of the heavy headdress. Clarissa gently attempted to pull it from Debbie's head, but her hair had tangled around it. "This would be easier to do if we could put her into the shower, wouldn't it?"

"Having a shower worked for Mr Sparky."

"Sharpy," Clarissa corrected him. "Yes, it did. Come on, let's try." She leaned over and spoke to Debbie loudly and clearly. "We think you'll feel better if we help you clean up, Debbie. Will you try for us?"

"Aaarrrrk!" was Debbie's only response.

That was good enough for Toby and Clarissa. Supporting Debbie on either side—Toby mainly supporting a calf muscle, to be fair—they led Debbie along her hallway and into her small but neat bathroom. Apart from the kitchen, the little one-bedroom flat was clean and tidy. All the walls were painted either white or cream, and the sparse furnishings in both the living room and the bedroom were grey. Everything seemed in order. Whatever Debbie had been up to over the past week or so, she hadn't been wrecking her own flat.

Clarissa peeled off Debbie's clothes and helped her under the shower, getting soaked herself in the process. Debbie seemed to shrink, forlorn under the beating water. Clarissa focused the shower head on Debbie's hair and started to work the headdress away, using a little conditioner in an attempt to work through some slip. Eventually she located a pair of nail scissors in the bathroom cabinet and resorted to using those to cut the worst mats free from the base of the headdress. Once she'd released it, she deposited it in the sink before attacking Debbie with shampoo.

When the water finally ran clear, Clarissa wrapped her in the towels that Toby had located in the airing cupboard, led her to her calm, quiet bedroom and set her down on the bed. "Put your feet up," Clarissa ordered, helping Debbie do just that. "I'll sort out the bathroom and make you some more tea, then we'll comb your hair out. You'll feel better soon, I promise."

Humming her little song—to Toby it sounded like an Eastern European folk song, or something that should be accompanied by balalaikas, at any rate—

Clarissa headed back to the bathroom to begin mopping up. Showering a zombie is a messy task! She began by retrieving the headdress from the sink. Turning it over in her hands, she marvelled at the intricacy. The flowers, as old as they were, had been individually crafted from brightly coloured silk and set onto a silver tiara studded with diamanté.

"Not real silver, though," Clarissa said, turning it over to see if there was a maker's mark.

There was.

"It *is* real silver. Wow."

"Must be worth a bit," said Toby, who only ever thought about the value of things in terms of the number of sammiches he could buy.

"In that case ... would you set artificial stones on a silver tiara?" Clarissa wiped off the small stones. Even in the artificial lighting in the bathroom, they had an impressive sparkle. They could be real, but Clarissa had no way of knowing.

And in any case, she'd lost interest. Because far more pressing than the composition of the tiara was the existence of a small metallic—probably also silver—label attached to the underside of the tiara with four teeny-tiny screws.

"Ugh!" Clarissa, upon reading the words engraved

there, threw the headdress back into the sink. It clattered loudly.

"What's the matter?" Toby asked.

"This ... this ... thing! Ugh!" Clarissa backed away.

"I thought it was rather nice." Toby was confused. He tried to stand on his back legs with his front paws on the edge of the sink. but he wasn't quite tall enough to see over. No matter. He'd been practising his levitation skills just for this sort of eventuality.

"Come," he said, training his thoughts on the headdress. "Rise and come to me." The headdress slid out of the sink and rose a few inches before dropping down in front of his face.

"Put it back, Toby! You have no idea where it's been."

"I know it's been on Debbie's head, for starters," Toby reminded her.

"For laters, more like. It's where it *started* life you need to worry about."

Toby focused on the silver tag that Clarissa had been reading. The problem for him was that the writing was titchy. The biggest letters at the top spelled out a name. "Mary Elizabeth Salcombe," he read. "What about her?"

"It says, 'Mary Elizabeth Salcombe, late of this parish'—"

"Late? She should be forgiven, surely? We all have our little foibles," said Toby.

"It means she died, Toby."

"Died?" Toby's eyebrows twitched. "Right, right. Poor lady."

"Mary Elizabeth Salcombe," Clarissa tried again. "Late of this parish, b:1732 d.1758. Beloved wife of Henry Arthur Salcombe. May she rest in peace."

Toby gazed quizzically at Clarissa with big brown eyes.

"It means Mary Elizabeth must have been buried in this."

"Ah," said Toby. "Then ... where did Debbie find it?"

Clarissa pulled a face. "My thoughts exactly!"

CHAPTER NINETEEN

"Goooood evening, witches everywhere."

Madam Redd's husky tones wafted out across the world, or at least everywhere anyone was able to tune in to her podcast, which is almost the same thing these days. Based in Tumble Town in the paranormal enclave tucked away behind Carnaby Street in London, Madam Redd hosted one of the most popular shows in streaming history. Her broadcast was an eclectic mix of music and special guests but with an emphasis on current affairs affecting witches, wizards and other magickal beings.

Toby cocked his head as she began to speak. Clarissa had kitted him out with a spare pair of earphones, and he was listening in through her laptop. She'd been reluctant to let him do this, but he'd been insistent—and to be fair, he'd been involved in this whole strange situation since the beginning, so she hadn't been able to deny him.

"We're going to start with this little vintage gem by Adam and the Ants, and then I have a very special guest for you, all the way from Devon." The intro to *That Voodoo* began to play and Madam Redd, turning the sound down, cut to Clarissa. "Just a few minutes and we'll be with you."

"I'm ready," said Clarissa. It had been a long day. An exhausting day. After leaving Debbie, she and Toby had hustled to the library to trawl through the records held there. Sadly, most of the paper copies had been moved to the main archive at Exeter, but the good news was that Clarissa could access them online, so she and Toby—who, much to his horror, had not been allowed into the library and had been forced to wait outside—had hurried home. Apart from fixing some cheese on toast, Clarissa had been working like a trojan ever since. She'd filed the first report about the zombie problem for her paper and, after a quick edit, it had gone live on *The Celestine Times*' website along with her video footage and some stills.

Within ten minutes, the producer of Madam Redd's podcast, *By the Pricking of My Thumbs*, had contacted Clarissa's editor begging for Clarissa to take a guest slot that very night.

Clarissa had been delighted to accept and now, both excited and nervous, her palms clammy and her heart beating a little fast, she waited for Madam Redd to come back to her.

"And there you are, my friends," crooned Madam Redd. "A thrill a day does indeed keep the chills away. And I'm going to chase your chills away this evening because, speaking of thrills, I am delighted to welcome Clarissa Page to the show. Good evening, Clarissa."

Clarissa cleared her throat of the frog that had suddenly appeared there. "Good evening, Madam Redd."

"Just call me Redd, darling. All my friends do." Redd's smooth, encouraging voice drifted down Clarissa's phone line. "Clarissa is the south-west region's correspondent for *The Celestine Times*. Do I have that right, Clarissa?"

"That's correct."

"And, as many of my more astute listeners will already know, just this afternoon you've been breaking a story about zombies in your home town of Sun Valley. Tell us about that."

Clarissa quickly and proficiently outlined the story. The locals who had complained to police about 'ravers', the absence of arrests and then the footage she had taken while in the Palais that clearly revealed half a dozen couples dancing to rock and roll. She opted to leave out Mr Sharpy, deciding that as he was well on the road to recovery, he didn't need to be bothered by any internet weirdos of the kind that doorstep the vulnerable.

Besides, that would have meant admitting she might have been at fault for spreading the virus further.

"That's quite some footage," said Redd. "With the blessing of *The Celestine Times*, we've put that on the website for everyone to see, so if you're one of the few listeners who hasn't viewed it yet, make sure you head to Madam Redd dot com. Like and follow us for more. And don't forget to subscribe! We're heading to a break now, and after that we'll listen to *Monster Mash* by Bobby "Boris" Pickett and the Crypt-Kickers, which seems rather fitting for this story. If you have any questions for Clarissa, you can contact us in the usual ways. Back soon!"

Clarissa breathed a sigh of relief as the faint sound of *Monster Mash* made its way into her ear.

Toby jiggled about on his chair. "This is a bop," he said loudly, not understanding that just because he couldn't hear his voice, didn't mean Clarissa couldn't.

Clarissa pressed her finger to her lips. "Sorry!" said Toby, so loudly that Mrs Crouch could probably have heard him through the walls.

Clarissa rolled her eyes and waited patiently until Redd came back on the line and the podcast began again.

"You said to me earlier that you tracked down one of the zombies today, Clarissa. Could you tell us more about that?"

"I was following a lead," said Clarissa, smirking at the double meaning of that—literally following Toby on a lead—"and while I don't want to give too much away about the person I located—"

"Understandably," said Redd.

"Yes. I did find something interesting that may well be a clue as to how this outbreak has occurred."

"Are you able to say much about that?" asked Redd. "I'm sure my listeners are dying to know more."

"I found something on this person that suggests she had somehow found some grave goods."

"Really?" Redd crooned. She was enjoying this. "How macabre. So, was this zombie undead? Had they been disinterred and come back to life?"

"I can categorically say that is not the case. I will say that this lady is now being looked after, and I hope she'll make a full recovery."

"So she was alive and she became a zombie?"

Clarissa hesitated. How much could she say? Or how much should she say? So far, Ed hadn't had any luck persuading his superiors that they should track down all the zombies from the Palais and isolate them. "That does appear to be the case," she admitted. "But I don't know where the source of the infection is."

For example, thought Clarissa, *I have no idea how Mr Sharpy became a zombie. Did he catch it from someone?*

"But it is the case that the construction site where these disturbances have occurred includes a church and an old graveyard—that's right, isn't it?" Redd pressed.

Drat. Clarissa hadn't expected Redd to 'bone' up on her research. "Yes."

"Implying that graves have been disturbed on the construction site, and somehow that's been enough to let loose some disease that's spawned a number of zombies in the Sunshine Valley area?"

Oops. "It's a theory," said Clarissa.

"Compelling stuff! Hang on right there, Clarissa. We're going to take another break for a message from our sponsor and listen to The Automatic singing *Monster*, and then we'll take some questions from our listeners."

Clarissa groaned and eased her back out of its cramped position as she switched off her mobile. It needed charging anyway, but she had a feeling that once Ed received word of what had been said on the podcast, he'd be trying to bend her ear.

"Coooooool, baby!" Toby, emulating Redd's soft, sexy drawl, pulled his earphones out. "Goooooooood job."

"Behave," Clarissa replied.

"Maybe I could launch a radio station in my wizard shack and do a Toby podcast? What do you think?"

"What do I think?" Clarissa laughed. "That it's probably way more work than you imagine!"

Toby ignored that. "You could be my first guest."

"Thanks." Clarissa stood and stretched. "Time for bed! I'm done in." She pointed towards the back. "Better do your final checks of the day."

"Yeaaaah, baby!" said Toby. "Heading out into the great unknown to explore the darkness ..."

"Just go."

"Alright, keep your hair on."

"I'm heading up." Clarissa yawned. "I'll turn the lights off as I go. See you in a minute."

Toby scuttled through his dog flap and charged up the garden. He stood on the lawn taking deep breaths of fresh air, head and tail high, listening to the sounds of the night. There were a few disturbances. Griffin, the poor Great Dane Toby had befriended when searching for the missing puppies, had been left out again. What were his owners thinking? Every night, it was the same old story. Toby felt sorry for him.

A couple of cats were scrapping up at number fifty-two, but it didn't sound like they were seriously trying to kill each other. Just a bit hormonal. Toby wondered if Moriarty was one of them.

"Ahem."

Toby glanced upwards. Moriarty, eyes glowing, stared down at him from the top of the wizard shack. *How dare she? She does know that's my platform, does she?* It hadn't been supplied as a free-for-all.

"I'm certainly not hormonal," Moriarty told him. "I've been done."

"Ah." Toby decided to skirt over this in the interests of delicacy's sake. But ... had she read his mind?

"You should come up here," said Moriarty.

Toby didn't need a second invitation. He carefully —he still wasn't sure about the steps—climbed up to the platform. "Scooch over," he said, and Moriarty moved her tail by a fraction of an inch. "A little more?"

Sighing in that disdainful way that female cats have, Moriarty moved over enough to allow Toby to plant his backside down. He sat straight, stretching his head, prepared to take in the starry skies over Devon.

"Do you see it?" Moriarty asked.

Toby followed her gaze. Over in the direction of town, Toby spotted lights shooting into the sky. Pink. Orange. Blue. "Fireworks?" he asked, although he couldn't hear any bangs.

"I don't think so," Moriarty answered. "This has been going on since it became dark, though."

"Wait." Toby watched the lights spin. "I've seen this on telly. Aren't these lasers?"

"Could be. But why? It's not Christmas."

"Might be a carnival," Toby said, although if there was due to be one in town, he'd have expected to know about it because all his friends would have been sharing the news. There were always plenty of sweets and treats to forage on the day after the carnival as long as you were there before the council's street cleaners.

"Where do you think they're coming from?" Moriarty asked. "The park?"

Toby thought about this. "Not far from the park, certainly. Maybe ... maybe the market." Pippin would know about that. He could find her and ask in the morning when he and Clarissa went back to the construction—

He caught his breath. What if these lights were coming from the construction site? What if the zombies were having a proper party with lights and all sorts?

What if there were more of them?

Toby glanced back at the house. The downstairs lights were out, but he could see Clarissa's silhouette in the bathroom. The window was open, and he could hear her using her electric toothbrush.

Should he run up and let her know what was going on?

No.

She was tired. And he didn't really know for certain, did he?

He'd mention it in the morning.

CHAPTER TWENTY

"Ms Page?"

Clarissa squinted at the figure at her door. Beside her, Toby poked his head out, unsure whether to bark or wag. Between the two of them it was a toss-up who looked the most tousled. Neither of them had been awake when the rat-a-tat-tat came at the door.

Clarissa tugged self-consciously at her pyjama top. As much as she liked it—covered as it was with teddy bears with wands and little witchy hats—she wasn't sure it was her first choice of apparel when answering the front door.

Especially when the person presenting themselves on the other side was wearing a sharp-looking, expensive suit in a kind of green-tinged grey, with a cream shirt and a charcoal-coloured silk tie.

"Mmm?" she said, trying—and failing miserably—to hold back a scowl.

Toby scowled along with her, not because he was wearing pyjamas—he wasn't—but just for the fun of it.

The man seemed unperturbed. "I'm extremely sorry to bother you at this time of the morning—"

"What time is it?" Clarissa asked, her voice gruff. Toby sympathised. They surely hadn't been asleep that long?

"Just after six."

"Six o'clock? Nobody should be knocking on my door this early." Clarissa peered across the road and then along the street, hoping that all the kerfuffle hadn't disturbed her neighbours. What on earth would they think?

"I know. As I say, I do apologise. I waited as long as I could." He held up the identity card on his lanyard. "Dr Robert Eerie from Kings College, London. I'm here at the behest of the Home Secretary."

Clarissa stepped backwards, standing on Toby's toe. "What? Why?"

"Yaooow!" Toby hopped around, tail between his legs.

Dr Eerie cautiously eyeballed Toby before turning

his attention to Clarissa once more. "I'm a biochemist and adviser to the UK government, so—"

"A biochemist?"

"Indeed."

"I don't need a biochemist today, thank you." Clarissa began to close the door.

Dr Eerie held his hand out and prevented her from doing so.

"Excuse me? Do you mind?" Clarissa exclaimed.

"I think you do need a biochemist—"

"No, I don't. I don't need a vacuum cleaner, religion, politics or charity, and I most certainly don't want the government on my doorstep. Thank you very much." Clarissa closed the door.

Dr Eerie wasn't going to be that easy to dissuade, however. He began to knock. "Ms Page?"

"If you don't go away," Clarissa said to the crack in the door, "I'm going to set my dog on you."

Beside her, Toby baulked at the idea. "Are you?"

"Yes."

"Please don't," Toby begged. "I'm a wizard, not a fighter."

"I thought the saying was 'lover'?"

Toby tossed his head. "That was in the old days. I'm not a puppy anymore."

"Ms Page. I can have you forcibly extracted, you know?" Dr Eerie's voice drifted through from outside.

"Can he?" Clarissa asked Toby, but Toby didn't have a clue.

"And I can have your dog removed."

"Removed?" Toby's ears disappeared, lying flat along his head.

"That's blackmail." Clarissa threw open the door. Toby bolted backwards, taking cover half in and half out of the living room. If necessary, he'd slip through his dog flap and seek sanctuary with Mrs Crouch.

"Who do you think you are?" demanded Clarissa, forgetting all about her pyjamas and disturbing the neighbours. "How dare you knock on my door and begin threatening me! I'll call the police!"

Dr Eerie smiled. "The police will have no jurisdiction in this matter, Ms Page. As I said, I'm here on the authority of the Home Office."

The reminder gave Clarissa pause. She had no idea whether what he was saying was true and that the police wouldn't intervene, but he sounded pretty sure of himself. "What do you want?" she asked testily.

"I'll come straight to the point. Your appearance on a certain podcast yesterday evening did not go unnoticed. In the interests of national security, I have been asked to interview you in order to verify the information you provided on said podcast and then take necessary action."

Clarissa folded her arms and glared at Dr Eerie. "I appreciate you've come a long way—"

"I have. I left London at two this morning, having been briefed on all pertinent matters and having watched the footage *The Celestine Times* uploaded onto their news site. I've been sitting in my car for an hour, listening and re-listening to the podcast and waiting for you to wake up ..."

"I didn't wake up," Clarissa reminded him. "*You* woke me up!"

"The sooner we can begin, the better. May I come in?"

"Absolutely not," growled Clarissa.

Toby growled along with her, but from the safety of the living room door.

"If I might remind you—"

Clarissa knew she was fighting a losing battle. "I know. I know! You have the authority of the British government and no doubt the king—"

"Undoubtedly." Dr Eerie curled his lips in a semblance of a smile.

"Let me put some clothes on."

"I'll wait in my car."

"I may be some time," Clarissa grumbled, determined to grab a shower and a coffee too.

"Don't be," ordered Dr Eerie, and backtracked towards the sleek black car parked by the kerb.

To Clarissa's consternation, when Dr Eerie pulled into Boyd's construction site, another three cars were waiting for them, each exactly the same as the one he was driving. Judging by the leather seats and the shiny paint, the little Union Jack flags on the windscreen and the diplomatic number plates, what she was seeing here was a fleet of ministerial cars.

King Street had been closed off, and, although it wasn't yet seven in the morning, crowds were gathering behind the temporary barriers. The gates to the construction site were already wide open—Clarissa spotted the bald receptionist standing around with his colleagues glumly watching a dozen or so uniformed police officers combing the area—and several people in lab coats and hard hats were waiting for them.

Clarissa jumped out of the car, pulling Toby behind her. Dr Eerie hadn't wanted to bring a dog along for the ride, but Clarissa had been adamant that she didn't go anywhere without him. Besides which, given that neither she nor Toby had a clue what was happening, they were loathe to be separated.

"Who are these people?" Clarissa asked, indicating the waiting lab coats.

"They're scientists from my lab. After your podcast last night, I thought it would be well worth testing soil samples here in situ to see what we have."

"So you're buying into this idea that the construction workers have disturbed the old graveyard, are you?"

"There has to be a centre of contagion somewhere. A nucleus. It's important we find out and take steps to eradicate it."

Clarissa nodded. She could see that made sense. But of course, Dr Eerie and his motley crew didn't know about Mr Sharpy, and she certainly wasn't ready to spill the beans yet. She wanted to see how events shaped up.

"Good morning, team," Dr Eerie addressed the white lab coats. "Sorry I'm a little later than scheduled. We were ... er ... held up." He looked pointedly at Clarissa.

Clarissa folded her arms and pressed her lips together. Toby moved in front of her, hackles rising.

"Perhaps we could leave the dog in the portacabin?" Dr Eerie suggested.

"Perhaps we couldn't," said Toby.

"No," said Clarissa. "He stays with me. At *all* times."

Dr Eerie sighed. "What updates do you have for me, Clemence?"

A beautiful black woman stepped forward. Tall and curvy, she might have been Beyoncé but with sleek tresses instead of loose curls. Despite the official white lab coat, there was something about her that set off Toby's tingles. It might have been the blue lipstick, or it might have been her curious and unusually green eyes ... green eyes like Moriarty.

"The local police have been searching the construction site since first light, Dr Eerie, but they've yet to find anything or anybody." She lifted her gaze from her notes and met Toby's gaze. "We have yet to find the plans for the church and churchyard—we haven't been able to wake anyone from the local council—although we did manage to download some aerial maps from the nineteen nineties that indicate the boundaries. The church was deconsecrated about eleven years ago, and after that it was used as a community space and a coffee shop. It's been out of use altogether for four years."

"Who does the land belong to now?"

"Travis Boyd Construction. The owner is Travis

Boyd himself. We've asked him to join us on-site this morning. He's travelling here from Bournemouth. We did a little digging, and it appears his company has been steadily buying all the buildings in this area for years."

"It's constructing a shopping centre. Is that right?"

"Yes." Clemence didn't pass comment, but something in her expression suggested disapproval. Clarissa noted it and looked at Toby.

A potential ally among these governmental jobsworths?

"We've checked out his licences and permits, and everything looks above board."

Dr Eerie nodded. "Very well. May I introduce you to Clarissa Page? She's the journalist from *The Celestine Times* who broke the story last night."

Clemence held out her hand. "Pleased to meet you."

Dr Eerie nodded at Clarissa. "This is Dr Raine Clemence from the University of Bath."

"Call me Raine." Raine's smile was as warm as her handshake.

"And this is Toby," Clarissa told her.

Raine stooped to scritch his ears. "Pleased to meet you too, young man. Have you been helping Clarissa with her story?"

"I do what I can," said Toby, pretending not to enjoy the fuss.

"I'm sure you do," said Raine, standing again.

Toby's jaw dropped. Proof, if proof were needed. Raine was one of them! A witch!

"Dr Eerie?" A young man with sandy hair and a trendy beard hurried over. "Mr Boyd has arrived." Toby and Clarissa turned to see an enormous four-by-four trundling through the gates. When it pulled up, a huge bear of a man jumped out, his shirt straining across his chest.

"I'll go and have a chat with him," said Dr Eerie. "Clemence, would you walk Ms Page around the site and map what she's seen and where?"

"Of course."

Raine smiled at Clarissa and Toby and indicated the direction of the old church. They began to stroll towards it. As soon as they were out of earshot, Clarissa cocked her head and widened her eyes.

Raine put a finger on her lips and kept moving. "Miss Page," she said, her voice carrying. "From the original footage supplied by one of the local residents, it seemed as though they were in this area, close to where the old graveyard was located ..."

Clarissa looked around. "That's right." She pointed at an area where the path sloped. The retaining wall had been taken away and the ground had crumbled, but you could vaguely make out the old topography. "You can see the fountain here. There was a paved area here, with benches against the walls."

"Old Joe used to bring me here," Toby chipped in. "He liked to sit here."

"Old Joe was my grandfather," Clarissa explained. "He made Toby spellbound so he can speak to witches."

"I speak to everyone," Toby clarified. "He made me spellbound so witches could understand me." He remembered The Pointy Woman. She'd have liked to take credit for Old Joe's extraordinary spell, but the truth will out.

"A wonderful magickal feat," Raine agreed. "And incredibly useful!" She scrutinised the area. "When you used to come here with Old Joe, could you see any gravestones? Can you remember any?"

"None on the grass, but there were a couple up against the wall," Toby told her.

"They were probably moved there when the ground was deconsecrated," Raine said, leading them over to the approximate location of where the wall would have been. "Oh, look!" Her sharp eyes picked out what to anyone else would have seemed like a random chunk of rock, but when she turned it over,

Clarissa and Toby could clearly see words engraved there.

"Surely the graves were moved too?" Clarissa asked.

"Oh, undoubtedly!" Raine agreed. "My only concern would be whether the council, or the contractor employed by the council to do the work, took any shortcuts."

"I see what you mean," Clarissa agreed. "From the research I've done, this was only a small graveyard, and the internments ceased around the time the big department store was built in the middle of the nineteenth century because they bought up the land. I suppose, back then, they protected the graves, but a hundred and fifty years later when the church and grounds were deconsecrated, there wouldn't have been many people left who'd have cared."

"That's my thought, too," said Raine.

"Can I ask ..." Clarissa hesitated, peering over her shoulder to see what Dr Eerie was up to. The head scientist was engaged in an animated discussion with Travis Boyd. "What do you intend to do with the zombies if you find them?"

Something passed over Raine's face. "I'm not able to discuss that at this time—" She broke off and moved away, heading towards the grand Victorian building that had once housed the Palais. Turning back to Clarissa, she asked, "Where do you think the zombies go during the day?"

Clarissa placed a hand on her hip. "I'm not able to discuss that at this time."

Raine stared at her, her expression hard. Toby wondered whether this encounter, which had been going so well, was going to turn sour.

"But you know?" asked Raine.

Clarissa shrugged.

Raine dropped her gaze to Toby. "My lips are sealed," he said, clamping his jaw closed.

Raine nodded. "Fair enough," she said. "Let's go through to the nightclub building, shall we?"

CHAPTER TWENTY-ONE

Clarissa and Toby snuggled on the sofa in the darkness. The television cast the only light in the room. They'd been sitting that way for nearly ninety minutes, watching a film and sharing popcorn. If anyone had asked them, neither of them would have been able to tell you what the film was about, but the popcorn had gone down a treat.

As the closing credits rolled, Clarissa sighed and whispered, "Raine was a strange one, wasn't she?"

"One of us and not one of us," Toby agreed. "Why are we whispering?"

"You don't mess with the government, Tobes. The whole house is probably bugged."

"Like Homeland!" Toby loved a bit of Claire Danes.

"But more British," Clarissa said. "Still ruthless, but they'll offer you a cup of tea." She laughed at her own joke and reached for the remote.

"We should go and sit on the platform. They won't have bugged us up there," Toby suggested.

"It's getting late," Clarissa said. The ten o'clock news was just starting. "We should probably turn in and try for a decent night's sleep. Maybe we'll come up with a plan in our dreams!"

"That would be—"

"Sssh!" Clarissa turned the volume up. "Is that where I think it is?"

The news cameras were trained on a reporter standing in front of a now-familiar-looking fence. Above her head, lasers were zapping through the sky like neon lightning. The reporter—their old friend Abbie McKnight—had one finger in her ear and was shouting into her enormous furry microphone.

"—has unexpectedly turned into ... well ... it's hard to describe, actually. A mega party. A rave for the over-fifties? One resident described it as a zombie jamboree, and in fact, hashtag zombie jamboree is trending on social media—"

Clarissa bolted to her feet. "I have to go down there!"

"Dr Eerie said you weren't allowed to," Toby

reminded her. Before they'd been dropped back home this afternoon, they'd been warned against leaving town *or* ever turning up at Boyd's Construction again. Apparently, Mr Boyd was considering gaining a stalking protection order against Clarissa. He blamed her for all the fuss.

Stupid man.

"Dr Eerie is not the boss of me!" Clarissa sniped.

"Nor me!" agreed Toby. "I'll come with you!"

"Despite the roads being closed off by the police earlier today, crowds of locals have started turning up." The camera spun around to take in men and women of all ages, along with some children and dogs lining the barriers. In the houses directly across the road from the building sites, residents were hanging out of their windows, many with their mobiles trained on the activity below.

The camera panned back to Abbie. "A source close to the government tells me that earlier today, the Home Office sent scientists to ascertain what's going on here—"

"I wonder who Abbie's source might be," Clarissa said, dashing out into the hallway to grab her boots.

"Clarissa! Look at this!" Toby called her back. "They have drone footage!"

Clarissa hurried back in and perched on the sofa.

Together, they viewed the television with disbelief. Where just two days ago there had been a dozen zombies, now there were over a hundred! They lurched around, waving their stiff arms, necks held at awkward angles, many looking like they'd thrown a disc in their lower backs. The thing was, they were having a whale of a time! Half a dozen of them even had glo-sticks, and, from the drone's vantage point, it appeared that someone had thrown several cans of paint around because the light from the lasers was picking out patches of yellow and orange and green.

"What in the eighties revival is going on?" Clarissa asked.

"Let's hurry down there and find out!" Toby bounced around excitedly. *Yes! Another adventure!*

Traffic was unusually heavy for the time of night. Clarissa and Toby walked into town, but cars were queuing in every direction, fighting for spaces in which to park. People were tooting horns and shouting, and there was a general feeling of hysteria.

And no wonder, really. Even as the pair approached the market they could hear the music pumping. Salt-N-Pepa's *Push It* blasted out around the town centre.

"Tune!" said Toby, waggling his butt in time to the beat.

"You were born in the wrong era, babe!" But even goth-band-loving Clarissa had some pep in her step.

A number of cars had cheekily parked on the marketplace, but without a parking warden in sight, there probably wouldn't be any penalties. People pushed past them from all directions. Blue light flickered against the buildings, reflected from police cars caught up in jams. Thanks to the gridlock around town, no-one in a vehicle was going anywhere—and that included the emergency services.

The burger van on the market was open and doing a storming trade. Toby sniffed appreciatively as they passed by, keeping an eye open for Pippin, but she didn't appear to be around. They continued walking up King Street, joining the throng heading that way and observing groups of young men trying to climb the fence either to see inside or to join in. Either was a distinct possibility.

Clarissa paused to watch before taking her camera out and starting to film. "Never let an impending disaster stand in the way of a juicy story," she muttered, and Toby could only ponder what she meant.

Impending disaster? Why?

For him, this was all a little boring. He was far too short to be able to see over the fence, naturally, although had Clarissa let him off the lead, he would have been able to find a gap and squeeze through, and that would have been much more interesting. Instead, he had to console himself by smelling the world. Lots of stale, meaty zombies. Lots of stale but not quite so meaty humans. Also, some rather more fragrant humans and others with cloying perfumes and colognes. Ugh. He hated artificial scents.

Ooh! Wait though! Was that *candyfloss* he could smell? He pulled Clarissa's arm. "Candyfloss!"

Clarissa steadied her arm. "Not now, Toby, we're working."

"Candyfloss makes me work harder."

Clarissa took her eye away from the camera. "When have you ever eaten candyfloss?"

"There's always a first time."

"It's pure sugar. It's not good for dogs. Now hush!" She turned back to her camera, angling herself slightly sideways as she followed a group of strong-looking lads as they climbed the hill, all wearing almost identical outfits of heavy working boots, canvas trousers with pockets and dark hoodies over jumpers. All that and the temperature had yet to dip beneath nineteen degrees. "Who are they? Young Farmers?" She chuckled, but the smile was wiped off her face when she realised what they were doing. "They're going for the main gate!"

"Uh-oh." Toby didn't need pulling; he instinctively knew Clarissa was going to be following them. He ran with her as she rushed up the hill, but it was almost impossible to close in on the gate with all the crowds jostling around them.

Clarissa lifted her camera above her head and began recording again, although this proved difficult as she was constantly being bumped from all sides. Up ahead someone began chanting, and the crowd took it up. "Let's go, zombies, let's go!"

Salt-N-Pepa gave way to Frankie Goes to Hollywood's *Two Tribes* and a roar went up. Half the crowd continued chanting while the other half began dancing along to the introduction.

"I don't like this," Clarissa said, and Toby could sense her fear. If she didn't like it—and he had to admit, he wasn't enjoying getting his paws crushed—then he didn't like it either. He dodged about, trying to see through all the legs, before realising they'd be better off standing in a doorway. He tugged at Clarissa's lead, pulling her to sanctuary. She stopped recording and went with him.

Once safely ensconced in the doorway, where there was less of a crush, Clarissa could see a little more. "Those lads are at the gate," she told Toby. "They're climbing it!"

There were shouts. Police were running up King Street and down from the road at the top. The crowd jeered.

Clarissa lifted her camera and began recording once more. "They're wobbling the gate. Trying to weaken it!" Clarissa said. "Oh my!"

A woman screamed. More shouting. Then a heavy clang.

"Oh no! The gate's collapsed. There are people underneath it!"

Toby tugged at Clarissa. "We should go!"

"I can't. I need to record what's happening!"

"I have a bad feeling about this," Toby admitted.

More screaming. Not just women, either. And suddenly, the tide of people changed direction. Instead of heading towards the gates, people began pushing away from them. At first slowly. Those trying to leave engaged in a strange dance with those attempting to find out what was happening, but word began to spread.

"The zombies are free!" someone shrieked.

"They're free?" others asked.

"Someone's let them out!" A definite raising of the level of hysteria.

"Do they eat human flesh?" one woman wanted to know.

"Of course they do!" a deep voice answered. "They're cannibals! They eat humans!"

Toby gazed up at Clarissa. "Do they?"

"Not these ones," she said. "I think they prefer tea and biscuits if I'm honest."

"And sammiches!"

"Those too."

"There's a guy up there saying they're contagious!" a young woman on the verge of fainting shouted.

"It's like leprosy!" said her friend.

The young woman screamed and swooned, and that was all it took to cause a stampede. People began running in all directions. Up the hill, down the hill, into the nightclubs. With so many people in one place, it was only natural that individuals would become blocked in or tangled up. In their panic, they pushed and fought. Bodies fell to the floor like tenpins; fists were flying. The air was full of shouting, swearing, shrieking and screaming. Some were begging for their lives ... to be saved from nothing at all.

Clarissa kept her camera pointed at the action, hardly able to believe what she was seeing. Toby stood at her feet, barking—"Stay away!"—if anyone ventured too close to them.

Someone—a police inspector—had managed to lay her hands on a megaphone. "Ladies and gentlemen!" her voice rang out. "Please be calm! There is nothing to—ooooh!" There was a clanking, picked up on the megaphone, and then a high-pitched screech and nothing more.

That was the straw that broke the camel's back. The crowd hurried to disperse, mostly in the direction of the marketplace. Meanwhile, over the fence, Frankie—in Sunshine Valley rather than Hollywood —cried, "Ow, ow!" in sympathy with the hundreds of people scrabbling about on the narrow streets, desperately striving to make their way home to safety.

"Craziness," muttered Clarissa, panning her camera upwards. There was a helicopter above them now. She didn't know whether it was a news helicopter or a police helicopter, but it had started making tight circles overhead.

As the crowd began to thin, Clarissa panned the camera up King Street and spotted a couple of white vans at the summit—and, if she wasn't much mistaken, a number of white coats. Dr Eerie and his team were here, too.

She tightened the focus, zooming in on Dr Eerie. He was on his phone, talking in rapid-fire sentences, occasionally gesturing at the construction site and at other times at the sky. Beside him, one of the white lab coats—not Raine—suddenly jerked backwards and pointed. Dr Eerie's eyes widened. Clarissa followed his gaze.

A zombie.

Dressed in a pale yellow shirt and brown corduroy trousers, it lurched out of the gateway—made easier by the absence of gates thanks to the Young Farmers—and paused there, its head tracking left and right.

The nearest police officer drew his taser, taking aim at the thing's chest, but from out of nowhere, Raine ran up to him and stood in his way, shouting angrily. Dr Eerie began walking towards her, gesturing in annoyance, but she yelled back at him. Clarissa couldn't make out what was said, but clearly Raine had the best interests of the zombie at heart. Or at least, better interests than anyone else.

Before Dr Eerie could reach Raine and the police officer, the original banana-shirted zombie was joined by a couple of friends. A woman with a pretty sundress and yellow hair, more straw-like than it perhaps should have been, alongside another male in jeans and a Weird Fish t-shirt.

Dr Eerie backed away, and the police officer, after checking with his colleagues behind him, went with him.

Only Raine stood her ground.

The three zombies ambled, in their stuttering fashion, straight for her, arms held up and out. The sounds of *Two Tribes* faded away and, for a moment, there was a kind of silence, with only the sounds of the crowds disappearing into the marketplace, the distant warble of police sirens, the irritating deep-throated whining of the helicopter and the stomp of dozens of zombie feet as more zombies streamed out of the gates, their heads moving unnaturally left and right to take in their surroundings.

Clarissa's stomach squeezed, and goose pimples spread out from her shoulders.

"Do you think we should rescue Raine?" Toby asked, pulling on the lead once more but, before Clarissa could answer, the music started up again. Bruce Springsteen began singing about American dreams and suicide machines and being born to run, and the zombies waved their hands in the air and jerked around.

Clarissa burst out laughing. Perhaps Raine heard

her, because she looked directly at the two of them still sheltering in their doorway. Clarissa shook her head. "I don't know why everyone is so afraid of these goons. It *is* a zombie jamboree! This lot wouldn't hurt anyone!"

But even as she said the words, a green truck covered in khaki netting pulled up at the top of the road, and men in matching khaki uniforms, reinforced helmets and gas masks, and carrying heavy rifles began piling out of the rear.

"What's going on?" Toby asked.

"They've brought in the army!" Clarissa whispered, her voice laden with dread. "Oh, no. No, no, no, no! There's going to be a massacre!"

CHAPTER TWENTY-TWO

Toby and Clarissa stood on the front step of their house, staring out at the Range Rover rolling down the road. On the opposite side of the street, Moriarty waited with her owners, her bright eyes unblinking. Next door, Mrs Crouch, wearing a pretty sunhat and wielding a pair of pruning shears, was also watching. She may well have been trimming her roses but it was a little early for gardening, even for Mrs Crouch. Perhaps she considered herself armed and dangerous.

Clarissa and Toby had been rounded up like cattle the previous night by the soldiers. Dr Eerie had spotted her and had confiscated her camera. No matter how much Clarissa had questioned the legality of this, it had made no difference. She'd been unceremoniously thrown into the back of a police van and returned home.

Now, this black Range Rover, with speakers attached to its roof, was driving around the streets informing the residents of Sun Valley that the town was under a curfew and that everyone must stay in their homes. Clarissa had been woken by the tinny announcements as they were broadcast along the main road at the end of her street, although she hadn't been able to comprehend what was being said.

But now, as the Range Rover ambled along her road, she knew.

Spinning on her heel, Clarissa marched into the living room and switched on the television. Toby lingered on the front step, exchanging glances with Moriarty. When the cat's owners finally disappeared into their own house, she strutted across the road and joined Toby by his front gate.

"I take it this has to do with what happened in town last night?" she asked.

"I think so," he said. "Did you see it on telly?"

"Some of it. The hoomans were glued, but they're not the sort of people to go out and investigate like yours is."

"Clarissa's proper fuming this morning. They took her camera away," Toby said.

"Is it true that the army was called in?"

"Yes, real-life soldiers. They're smaller than they look in the films, but the guns are ginormous."

"And did they shoot all the zombies dead?" Moriarty asked, her tone nonchalant.

"What? No! Where have you been hearing this stuff?"

"On the Catvine, of course." Moriarty chuckled. "I took it all with a piece of salt."

"Pinch," said Toby.

"Pinch?" Moriarty repeated. "Why? Is it the first of the month? Rabbits, rabbits, rabbits!"

Toby danced around. "Where? Where? Let me at 'em!"

Moriarty snorted. "So you're not all peace and love when it comes to rabbits, are you?"

Toby plonked his bottom down and lifted a hind leg, all the better to scratch an ear with. "I don't know what you mean."

Moriarty mirrored him by cleaning a paw. "Are you going to tell me what happened?" she asked between licks. "Because if I'm going to be spreading gossip, I'd like it to be accurate."

"Sure. Well ... the zombies were having a party—"

"With cake?"

"I don't think there was cake. In fact, I don't think

there was any food whatsoever, although the burger van in the marketplace was doing big business, and so were the takeaways." Toby licked his lips. Clarissa would never let him have any curry, but oh boy, it always smelt so good! "There was lots of music and lots of dancing—"

"Yes." Moriarty blinked. "I gathered as much from the telly."

"Then the crowd went a bit mad and there were these hefty blokes—Clarissa said they were young farmers—and they broke the main gate down and the zombies spilled out and the police came and there was lots of shouting and a helicopter and—"

"And breathe?" suggested Moriarty helpfully, watching Toby's hind leg scratch faster and faster. He wouldn't have any ear left at this rate.

"It was very exciting," said Toby, sitting up straight. "Then the army came and they had the enormous guns. Huge guns. I mean. The guns were bigger than the soldiers. And they started rounding the zombies up and the police pushed all the bystanders away and then Clarissa was kind of arrested but not really ..."

This puzzled Moriarty. "How does that work?"

"The police told her we were trespassing and we'd be arrested, and then this Eerie fellow from the government came over and said he'd bring us home, so he did."

"Is the eerie man a zombie, too?" asked Moriarty.

"No. He's a scientist and he's investigating the zombies."

"Got it." Moriarty made a mental note. "And what does he intend to do with all the zombies?"

"I don't know," Toby replied, his voice sorrowful. "And neither does Clarissa, and that's making her cross!"

"I see. Are you sure she's not cross for another reason?"

"Like what?" Toby asked, wondering what Moriarty knew.

"Remember you asking for information about the man with the van who Clarissa has been seeing?"

"Yes?"

"Well, I have mews ... and it doesn't concern an aging mother with a curtain pole problem ..."

Clarissa had stormed back inside and turned the television on. While the news anchor covered the previous night's events, Clarissa boiled the kettle and filled the cafetière. Today was going to take a shedload of coffee. Slopping milk into her mug, she carried it and the cafetière into the living room to sit on the sofa and seethe in comfort while she re-caffeinated.

The local politician made an appearance, standing in front of the Boyd Construction sign to explain to local residents exactly why they were being prevented from leaving their homes.

"This is only affecting the residents of Sun Valley," he told the journalist—not Abbie, who must have been having a lie-in, but some young man in a cream suit—"and it's a temporary measure while the relevant authorities take stock of the situation. We want to make sure that everyone remains safe."

"Do you think it's a little drastic to close the schools and the supermarkets?" the journalist asked. "Standing here in Sun Valley you can hear how quiet it is, with all the business closed." The camera panned to demonstrate how quiet King Street was, firstly looking down the hill to the market, then back up to the main road. One of the local authority's distinctive yellow-and-orange-liveried buses drove past the top end.

"As I say, it's a precautionary measure. The government is taking the risk to the public very seriously—" the politician warbled.

The journalist interrupted. "Does the government

have any knowledge about these zombies and where they came from?"

The politician held up a hand—the thumb pressed into his fist in that peculiar manner politicians have, these days—and shook his head. "Giles, it would be wrong to make assumptions about these people—"

"The zombies, you mean?"

"You and I both know that zombies don't exist in reality, and we shouldn't be alarming the public—"

"So, the official line is that these aren't zombies?"

"I'm ... I'm saying that we don't know who these people are or what's going on, and it would be wrong of us to make assumptions."

Clarissa narrowed her eyes. What was afoot here? Was the government downplaying all that was happening? If so, why had the authorities decided to lock the town down?

Until this moment, it hadn't occurred to Clarissa that anyone was covering anything up, but now that it had, her mind began whirring. She jumped up.

Giles the journalist pressed on. "What's happening to the zombies—"

"People," the politician suggested.

"What is happening to *those* who were rounded up last night?"

"They are being kept on-site—"

"On this *construction* site behind us?"

"Indeed. The government is placing substantial resources into this temporary camp, including scientists and doctors and nurses. We're collecting blood samples and trying to ascertain exactly what has caused this mystery cold virus."

Clarissa stamped a foot. *Mystery cold virus*! There you had it. A complete spin by the Home Office.

"Everyone saw the footage of them dancing. Everyone knows they're zombies!" Clarissa bellowed at the TV.

Her mobile began ringing. She snatched it off the coffee table. Ed. "Hey!"

"Hi. Are you alright? Seen the news?" Ed asked, his voice quiet so that she had to concentrate to hear him. She reached for the TV remote and turned it down.

"Yes and yes. A bit peeved about last night."

"What happened? You weren't at the construction site, were you?"

"Of course I was. Where else would I have been? I was filming for *The Celestine Times* but I had my camera confiscated, was threatened with arrest, and then we were bundled home like a pair of criminals by the Home Office scientist!"

"Oh, dear."

"What about you? Were you there?"

Ed made a noise that sounded like an explosion of weariness and disgruntlement combined. "No. I raised concerns with my line manager, mentioned the zombies and he took it up the chain—an hour later I was summoned to the big chief's office. The long and the short of it, for spreading dissent, I am now confined to desk duty while they investigate *me*. That's why I can't talk very loudly. I'm in the corridor at the station, but there are plenty of people coming in and out."

"Oh, no, Ed!" Clarissa clamped a hand to her mouth and spoke through her fingers. "I'm so sorry! If I'd known this would happen, I'd never have involved you!"

"Don't be daft!" said Ed. "It might not be career-ending—" He laughed, but Clarissa sensed his dismay. "And anyway, it makes me angry that you can present people with the facts and they refuse to take any of them on board."

"I've just seen the local MP on the news. It looks like they're re-spinning it. Not zombies but a virus. Something akin to a heavy cold! Something stinks here, but I don't know what. They're focusing on the zombies on the construction site, but—"

"But?"

"There's a fly in the ointment," Clarissa said,

aware that everything they were saying might be overheard by secret agents but needing to tell him anyway. "You recall ... Toby's friend?"

"Toby's ...?"

"His *friend*, yes."

Ed took a moment, but the penny dropped. "Oh, right. Yes. Toby's 'friend'. He didn't need a ... a 'vet'. You sorted him out."

"That's right. Bless him. I haven't seen him for a while. I hope he's doing okay." Clarissa sat down in front of her laptop. "He's an outlier, Ed. Something is going on. It's being covered up."

"What do you mean?"

"I mean ... the council, local politicians, the government ... Maybe something besides the whole zombie outbreak."

There was a long pause. Ed bade someone a good morning. When he came back on the line, his voice was quieter than before. "I'll do some digging into Boyd's Construction. See what I can find out."

"Good idea," Clarissa said. "People need to know the truth, whatever that truth is." She grimaced. "I'm so annoyed! Apart from anything else, I had great footage from last night. You could *see* that the figures coming out of the gate were zombies, not people with blooming colds!" She flipped the lid of her laptop open. It whirred into action straight away. "I could have made it viral. I could—" She caught her breath.

"What?"

Clarissa jammed the phone between her ear and her shoulder and began violently hitting keys.

"Are you still there?"

"Yep. Still here. Give me a sec."

"What's going on?"

"I spent an absolute arm and a leg on that new camera when I first accepted the job at *The Celestine Times*. I haven't had much of an excuse to use it. Just bits and bobs and a few interviews and things. But if I recall, when I was going through the user instructions, it automatically uploads all your images and videos to the cloud!"

"Of course! Game changer!"

"Hang on." Clarissa began searching folders until she found what she was looking for. A folder she'd created and named 'Clarissa's Jazzy Camera Contents'. There, in a file marked with yesterday's date, were her photos and videos from the day before. "Whoop! There it is!"

"So what's the plan?"

"I'll send these to *The Celestine Times*." Clarissa stopped, chewing the side of her mouth as she considered the repercussions. "There's going to be fallout," she said, almost to herself. "Dr Eerie, the Home Office scientist, will know that these images came from me. They'll come for us, me and Toby."

"You'll have to go into hiding," Ed said, without a second's hesitation.

"But where can I go? They've closed the town down. They'll be watching the roads."

"They can't watch *all* the roads," said Ed.

CHAPTER TWENTY-THREE

"What—" Toby began to ask, but Clarissa put a finger to her lips. Raising her eyes to the ceiling, she waved the same finger round in a circle and finally tugged at her ear.

"Do you want some breakfast?" Clarissa asked. "I've had mine."

"What is it?" Toby asked, ever hopeful of sossidges and a bit of bacon. He wouldn't have said no to fried bread or an egg either, although he wasn't that keen on mushrooms and tomatoes.

"Schnauzer snacks," said Clarissa, and began disconnecting her laptop and gathering up various chargers and notebooks. "Help yourself."

Toby meandered through to the kitchen. When Clarissa said help yourself, she meant to what was in his bowl. She wouldn't take too kindly to him cooking a full English. He noted she'd packed some of his mixer and placed a few cans on the worktop. Judging by Clarissa's frantic activity, they were going on an illicit jaunt.

Pawesome!

Toby tucked into the contents of his bowl with gusto. You never knew where your next meal might come from when you were on the road. Where were they off to? Spain, maybe? Or somewhere like Nepal? Ooh! South America would be cool. Once his bowl was empty and he'd filled up on water, he salsa'd back into the living room, where Clarissa was pulling on her walking boots. Her backpack was stuffed full.

She put a finger to her lips once more and turned up the volume on the television. The morning news had given way to something a little chattier—although a doctor was talking about viruses, so it wasn't altogether off the subject—but she didn't sit down to watch it. She stood back from the window but strained her head to see out of it, then walked to the front door, Toby at her heels, treading quietly. He watched as she slipped the deadlock on and pulled the chain across. Again carefully, she lifted Toby's lead from its hook and wrapped it around her hand so it wouldn't jangle.

She indicated the back door, which stood open

and, after she'd grabbed her backpack, they made their way outside and up the garden behind Toby's wizard shack. The fence at the back of their garden badly needed replacing, so it was easy enough to quietly remove a couple of planks. Clarissa pushed the backpack through and Toby followed it, then she squeezed after him and did her best to replace the planks.

Fortunately for them, the garden behind theirs belonged to an old couple who rarely left the comfort of their front room and weren't big gardeners, so Clarissa and Toby were able to stealthily scramble along the edge of their boundary and round to the side gate. Once they'd let themselves out, they were home and dry.

Ish.

The next challenge was to make it to the end of this road, walking in the opposite direction to town towards a football field. This was a walk they occasionally did—although not usually through their neighbours' garden—just for somewhere different to explore. At the far end of the football field, the land gave way to trees and farmland. If you walked far enough through the wood you eventually came to what passed as a main road in East Devon, although it wasn't much wider than a large track.

Using the wood as cover, they walked in silence for

a good twenty minutes, perhaps longer, until finally Toby deemed it safe to speak. "Where are we going?"

"We need to travel far enough out of town that there won't be any checkpoints," Clarissa told him. "The authorities don't want people leaving, but if they don't see us go, they won't know, will they?"

"I'm always up for a good long hike!" Toby was pleased.

Clarissa burst his balloon. "We're not going on a hike. I've got too much to do."

"Are we camping?" Toby asked hopefully. Not as good as hiking, but exciting all the same.

"Nope." They'd come to the road at last. Clarissa peered up and down it. Deserted. Sticking to the edge of the tree line, she led Toby further up, in the direction away from Sun Valley, until they were adjacent to a bus stop. "I'm going to hide in here. I want you to wait by the bus stop. Tell me when a bus comes, and we'll stop it at the last minute."

"What if the buses aren't running?" Toby asked.

"They are. I saw one on the news this morning. They might not be picking up in Sun Valley, but they're probably still running between Exeter and the villages."

"Wowser," said Toby, meandering over to the bus stop to check for pee-mails and leave a few of his own.

Then he settled on the pavement and stared into the distance, waiting for the next stage of this strange adventure.

"Sergeant Major Sparky?"

"At your disposal, sir!"

Despite a strange look from the bus driver, Clarissa and Toby hadn't experienced any problems on the ride up to Bushy Leaze. Clarissa purposely stayed on the bus for an extra stop and then doubled back—wary that someone might be following them.

When that didn't appear to be the case, they made their way to Mr Sharpy's house and up the path to the front door. Sparky was the first to greet them, pleased as ever to see Toby and, of course, Clarissa, who had been so instrumental in making his poorly dad better.

"Mr Sharpy?" Clarissa called through the front door.

"Cwooooar!" came an answering cough, and Clarissa frowned, but it was followed by a friendly, "I'm in here. Come on in," so she unlaced her boots and pulled them off, leaving them at the front door. They found Mr Sharpy in the kitchen, watching the kettle begin to steam.

"How are you, Mr Sharpy?" Clarissa asked, examining the colour of his skin. He was pale, but the green tinge had completely disappeared.

"Getting better every day," he said. "It's good of you to come around and check on me."

"To be honest," Clarissa said, dropping her backpack on the floor and nudging Old Pete out of the way, "I badly need your help. Let me make the tea, shall I? You go and sit down."

"No need—"

"There's every need!" Clarissa scolded. "If I look after you, maybe you'll help me out."

"You don't even need to ask, I'm happy to help," Old Pete said. "One good deed deserves another." Nonetheless, he made his way into the living room while Clarissa popped teabags into the teapot and poured the hot water over them. Taking a spoon, she began to mash the brew, humming the song she always used.

Toby cocked his head, listening. Such a pretty tune.

Once Clarissa was happy, she carried the teapot and two mugs through to the living room and set them down on Mr Sharpy's small dining table before going back to collect some milk, the sugar bowl, a couple of teaspoons and her backpack. Juggling everything with great aplomb, she came to sit opposite Mr Sharpy and smiled at him. "Just a moment for the tea," she said, unbuckling her backpack. "Have you seen the news this morning?" she asked.

"I have! What a complete to-do." He held his right hand out, palm down, turning his fingers into claws. "I was one of them, wasn't I?"

"You were," Clarissa said. "And somehow, by some miracle, we made you well again."

"Can you do the same for all those poor people in Sun Valley?" Mr Sharpy asked. "There's an awful lot of them."

"I'd like to be given the opportunity to try, but it seems to me that people who genuinely want to help are being pushed out. I don't know why." Clarissa reached into her backpack and removed her battered notebook from the top. She smoothed it out on the table.

"How can I help?" Mr Sharpy asked.

"I want you to take me back to the few days before you became ill. I tracked down one of the victims who became ill after you—possibly after contact with you—"

"Oh no! I'm so sorry!"

"Don't worry—the last time I was able to check, she was on the road to recovery too."

"That's a relief." Mr Sharpy took a deep breath. "I'd hate to think—"

"Don't." Clarissa reached out and took his hand. "You can't blame yourself for something you had zero control over. You'll be doing a huge service if you can help me to get to the bottom of what's happening, and"—she squeezed his fingers—"help me work out why I wasn't infected too!"

CHAPTER TWENTY-FOUR

"You know I've spent an awful lot of time over the past few days trying to figure out why it happened to me," Old Pete said. Sparky came over to sit beside his dad and lay his head on his foot.

Toby, who couldn't be doing with such outward displays of emotion in public, climbed onto one of the two spare chairs so he could properly join in the conversation.

"And wondering whether I should notify the authorities in case I can be of any use to them," Old Pete continued.

"My dad's a good man," said Sparky. "He likes to do the right thing."

"But there's doing the right thing and acting in your own best interests," Clarissa said, once Toby had translated. "I'm not sure the two are mutually conducive in this case."

"Really?" Old Pete asked, reaching for the teapot.

His hand shook a little, so Clarissa took over. "Let's just say I remain to be convinced." She poured his tea. "Take me back to those last few days."

Old Pete wrapped his hands around his mug. Despite the warmth of the day, he shivered. "There are only two days I fully remember," he said, "according to what you've since told me about what I did and how long I slept."

Clarissa nodded.

Old Pete glanced at Sparky. "We start each day with a cuppa and then we go for our walk. Some days we drive to the beach, other times we like to walk around the old Rossiter's mansion. Do you know it?"

"I do." Rossiter's mansion had once belonged to a local family who had been wealthy industrialists during the latter half of the nineteenth century. They'd been instrumental in bringing work to Sun Valley and had been well loved. The family had moved to the USA in the nineteen forties, and over the years the mansion had been used as a hospital, a school and then council offices, but now the upkeep was too expensive and it had been left to gradually decay.

In Clarissa's opinion, it was only a matter of time

before some construction company bought the land and some chancer set fire to it.

Entirely unconnected, of course.

"It's derelict now. All boarded up. But a fascinating building. I've known it in its various guises my entire life. There's something about a building like that that keeps you grounded. It reminds you you're alive."

"Can you go inside?" Clarissa asked. Perhaps this was where the zombie virus stemmed from.

"I suppose some youngsters manage to find a way, but the last time I did so, it housed the local registry office." Old Pete chuckled. "I wasn't getting married; I was after a copy of my birth certificate."

"When would that have been?" Clarissa asked.

"Ooof. Fifteen, twenty years ago." He grunted. "Time flies."

"Wow." Clarissa raised her eyebrows. "And so now you just walk around the grounds?"

"Yes. I love it at this time of year. The council's gardeners do some work so there are some lovely flower displays, but most of it's just left to grow wild. It's good for the bees."

"And after your walk, what do you do?"

"Mostly we just come home and have some toast. I'll do some reading—"

"Have a nap," Sparky said.

"Naps are important," Toby agreed.

"Make a spot of lunch. Occasionally, in the afternoon, I'll drive to the shops."

"Did you do that on either of those days you can remember?" Clarissa asked.

"I vaguely recollect doing so on the day I first felt poorly. I had a terrible thirst."

Clarissa recalled the goods on the counter when she'd first come into the house. The empty cartons of juice. That made sense.

"I like to cook an evening meal. Something nourishing and tasty. When you reach my age, you don't want so much to eat, but what you *do* have needs to taste good."

Clarissa nodded. So far, she'd drawn a blank.

"You didn't go anywhere else? Take Sparky for a walk anywhere else?"

"No. Just Rossiter's."

Toby dropped his head to peer under the table. "Sparky? Do you play in the park? Play with other dogs?"

"I'm fifteen years old," Sparky reminded him. "Who wants to play with an old man like me?"

"Do you meet other dog owners?" Clarissa asked, taking up Toby's thread.

"Oh yes," Old Pete said. "That's one of the highlights of my day. We meet so many regulars. Some we exchange greetings with, others we might have a longer chat with. I know all the dogs by name." Old Pete chuckled. "Not so much the owners."

"You have your priorities right," Toby told him.

Clarissa was still thinking. "Did Sparky take anything off anyone that day? Or did he dig anything up?"

Sparky raised his head from Old Pete's foot. "I would *never* take sweets from strangers."

"Stranger danger," Toby agreed. "Although I myself am guilty of running off with someone else's ball."

"That's the worst!" Sparky exclaimed. "You should be court-martialled for that."

"No, we tend not to share treats or toys," Old Pete said.

"There was that woman though," said Sparky.

Toby's ears pricked up. "What woman?"

"Woman?" Clarissa echoed. "Did you meet a woman, Mr Sharpy?"

Old Pete stared down at Sparky, sprawled against his foot. "Oh, there was a woman. Messy."

"A messy woman?" Clarissa finally had something to write in her notebook.

"No. *She* wasn't messy as in scruffy. Far from it.

Smart-looking, in fact. From a distance. I didn't venture that close to her. No, what I mean ..." He scrunched his face up, trying to recall through the haze of a horrible experience. "She was sitting on a bench—one of those memorial benches dotted around the grounds. This one was at the front of the house. It has the best view of the grounds. She ... oh, that's right!" Old Pete smiled. "Messy, because she left her litter lying around."

"Litter." Clarissa leaned forward. "Did you ... touch it?"

"Of course. I picked it up and put it in the bin!"

"What exactly was it?"

"I imagined it was her lunch." Old Pete sniffed deeply and sat back. "It was odd, now you come to mention it. It was a bag. A white bag, stiff paper. Nothing written on it. No branding. The top had been folded over, so when I reached down to pick it up—and that took a bit of effort on my part because, you know, old bones have the least elastic—I expected there to be something in it. Why else close the bag up? But it was like a pillow of air. Nothing in it."

"Did you open it to check?" Clarissa asked.

"I did. Nothing in it *at all*. Not even a crumb, let alone a crust. Not a smidge of mayonnaise or a smear of butter."

Clarissa pursed her lips.

Old Pete shrugged. "As I say, just an empty bag. Hardly worth mentioning at all."

"And yet," Toby placed a paw on the table. "It's the only thing out of the ordinary ..."

"And must therefore mean something," Clarissa finished for him.

Clarissa felt rubbish asking, but the next time she made Old Pete a cup of tea, she broached the idea of staying with him. "It's a huge favour, I know. And a real cheek! The thing is, people may be after me and I need a base. Toby and I are perfectly happy to crash on your sofa, if you're agreeable. All I need is a blanket."

"And me," said Toby. "Although I'd quite like a pillow too."

"Hush you," said Clarissa.

"Hashtag just sayin'!" insisted Toby.

"Don't be silly," said Old Pete. "I have two spare bedrooms upstairs. You can use one of those!"

"We wouldn't want to put you out—"

"Nonsense. I'll enjoy the company. In fact, it'll be nice to cook for two—"

"Three," said Toby.

"Four," added Sparky.

"For a change." Old Pete flexed his hands. "I haven't had a proper dinner since I was poorly, so it gives me an excuse to be back in the kitchen. You make yourself at home, Clarissa."

"I'd like to do some work on my laptop, if you wouldn't mind?" Clarissa asked. "I took some footage of the activity on King Street last night and I'd like to send it to my editor."

"There's a socket behind you," Old Pete said, and tottered out towards the kitchen to investigate his cupboards, Sparky close behind him.

"Perfect." Clarissa began pulling wires and chargers and mice and hard drives and all the necessary accoutrements she would need for an afternoon's work from her backpack. As she set about plugging things in and switching things on, Toby watched her.

"What's the plan?" he asked.

"I'm going to review all the footage I took last night and edit together a piece to send to the office."

"Do you think it's time to tell the world about Old Pete?" Toby asked.

"Absolutely not. His safety is paramount. Besides, what have we got? There's no definitive proof that that bag he found contained anything harmful. While it looks likely to me that Old Pete is the source of the zombie virus, and poor old Debbie passed it on to more customers and members of staff at Goober's, I'm still not sure we have the whole story."

"Is it time for me to have a nap?" Toby asked, pondering on whether he should try to sneak a treat from Old Pete, but he didn't want to tread on Sparky's paws in his own kitchen. That would be the height of rudeness.

"I'd say that's a great idea." Clarissa began the painstaking job of going through the previous day's footage. First she watched the whole thing, then she began to splice down the component parts. The crowds. The fence. The burly lads. The police. The attack on the gate. The zombies stepping outside the building site. The panic. People fleeing. The soldiers. Raine. More footage of soldiers with their scary rifles and scarier gas masks.

Once that was done, she could create a narrative and pick and choose the pieces of film to include. Only then would she record her thoughts as a voiceover.

Ninety minutes in, she was selecting a few frames of the soldiers walking menacingly towards the broken gate and surrounding the zombies when Old Pete came back into the living room. "Sorry to disturb you," he said, and Clarissa smiled at the sight of him in his apron, his sleeves rolled up and a smudge of flour on his face.

Toby raised his head from where he'd been snoozing on the dining chair and yawned.

"I made you a cup of tea."

"That's smashing, thanks!"

Old Pete brought it over and placed it carefully on a coaster, peering over Clarissa's shoulder. "This is last night, is it? I saw the soldiers on the news this morning."

The camera angle panned back. On the laptop's screen, the footage focused on Dr Eerie and Raine Clemence. Clarissa clicked the mouse to stop it. The picture froze. She began to wind it back, intending to cut it after the soldiers, unsure whether she intended to mention the Home Office or Dr Eerie and his team in her video.

"That's her."

"Who?" Startled, Clarissa let the footage run back too far.

"The woman I saw at Rossiter's mansion. The one who left her rubbish behind."

"I thought you said you didn't get that close to her?"

Toby leaned over to see who they were discussing. *Dr Clemence?*

"I didn't. But I'd never seen her before, so she stood out to me ... and she had this aura ... I don't even know ... Sorry, I'm probably making no sense."

"It's fine." Clarissa froze the picture. "You're absolutely sure it was this woman?"

"Completely." Old Pete leaned closer to the screen. "So attractive. Something magnetic about her. Shining? Is that a good description? So beautifully turned out. You don't often see women taking such pains with their appearance these days." Old Pete smiled at Clarissa. "Not that I'm suggesting ..."

Clarissa pulled at her ponytail a little self-consciously. She couldn't remember whether she'd bothered to drag a comb through her hair this morning. "Mmm."

"Would you like a biscuit?" Old Pete asked, straightening up. He'd identified Dr Clemence but wasn't remotely concerned about it. He didn't suspect her of anything. Meanwhile, Clarissa's heart was racing.

"I'd love a biscuit," said Toby.

Clarissa cut her eyes at him. "That would be lovely, thanks," she said, her voice slightly faint.

As Old Pete headed for the kitchen, Clarissa slumped over the laptop, her forehead between splayed fingers, staring at the screen and the frozen image of Raine. "I don't understand."

"What's to understand?" Toby asked. "If we believe Mr Sparky—"

"Sharpy—"

"Old Pete. If we believe him, and I do, then for some reason Raine started this."

Clarissa scrunched up her face. "Maybe it was her packed lunch. Maybe there was something else that set this off, that Mr Sharpy can't recall."

Toby disagreed. "It's too much of a coincidence."

Clarissa nodded. "But why would she do it?" That was the burning question, and to that, they had no answer. "What do I do now? Who do I tell?"

"We must know someone," Toby insisted. "What about Grace Catesby?" Grace had been Clarissa's mentor at her old school, Ravenswood Hall.

Clarissa frowned and nodded at the same time. "She won't be able to do much but she might know someone who can. I'll drop her an email; see what she suggests."

"Maybe the Ministry of Witches?" Toby suggested.

"I don't know anyone there, but I could use one of their generic enquiries email addresses, I suppose. They would be able to put me in touch with the right people." Clarissa began to hammer away on her keyboard. She clicked the mouse a few times, swapped windows, copied and pasted a few things and added a couple of videos. Toby could only sit back and admire the speed at which she worked. He occasionally borrowed Clarissa's laptop to order new books—and *shhh*! snacks, but don't tell anyone—or to look up spells and ingredients, but he certainly couldn't type like a machine, the way she did.

Someone knocked on the door.

Sparky barked.

Clarissa and Toby both stiffened.

"I wonder who that could be," said Old Pete from the hallway. "I'm not expecting anyone. It's a full house today."

Clarissa was on her feet. "Don't open it!" She rushed towards the living room door, hoping to intercept him.

Too late. "Oh," exclaimed Old Pete. "We were just talking about you."

Clarissa bolted backwards, wanting to finish the email, but Raine appeared in the doorway, pushing Old Pete ahead of her. "Stay where you are," she said, "or I'll finish him off." She jabbed a long, twisted wand into the old man's neck, the point sharp enough to draw blood.

Sparky leapt up at her, barking as savagely as he could muster. "It's alright, Sparky." Old Pete, one hand to his throat and the other reaching for his dog, tried to calm the situation.

"Let me at her!" roared the fierce Yorkshire terrier. "I'll end her days!"

Toby barked. "Quiet, Sergeant Major!"

Sparky shivered, as much with anger as fear, and huddled close to Old Pete's feet.

Clarissa, totally flummoxed, held a hand up to Raine. "I don't understand! I assumed you'd come down with Dr Eerie to help with the zombie problem."

Raine sneered. "As if that old crock would ever be able to sort out a zombie problem! The government doesn't know its backside from its elbow."

"But you did this!" Clarissa cried. "You're responsible. You caused the first outbreak!"

"She caused it?" Old Pete asked. "How?"

"Whatever was in that paper bag is my guess," said Clarissa.

"Microscopic specimens of an active zombie virus I managed to obtain from ..." Raine smiled. "Let's just say I obtained them from a secret source who needs to remain nameless. They retrieved the samples from a laboratory in ... a former Soviet state."

Toby, still perched on his dining room chair, inched a little closer to Clarissa's laptop.

"But why Sun Valley? Why Mr Sharpy?"

Raine shrugged. "It was arbitrary. I was looking for a small town on or close to the coast, so that once the virus began spreading, it would be easier to contain. I needed a single victim because I didn't want mass exposure to the virus at first. I wanted to monitor how quickly it spread. With that sort of data, any virus can become a weapon of war. It's a lucrative business."

Raine chuckled. "If I'm honest, I picked Sun Valley because the name appealed to me. And I picked the location, in the grounds of that dilapidated mansion, because that's the only place I could find somewhere to park."

Sparky whimpered.

"The problem was, I dropped the package and moved away to keep watch from a distance but was distracted by a phone call. I lost Mr Sharpy in the park and was unable to keep tabs on him. Entirely regrettable. I only knew the plan had worked when the first zombies appeared on the news." Raine grinned. "Thanks to your stellar reporting, of course."

"You could have killed people!" Clarissa protested. "If Toby and I hadn't located Mr Sharpy, he'd have died here alone!"

Raine shrugged. "That's a sacrifice I was willing to make. There's money to be had in germ warfare. An awful lot of money. There are groups all over the world who pay in gold bullion for even the sniff of a virus."

Clarissa choked. "That's evil."

"It's capitalism!" Raine spat. "Do you know how much a university lecturer earns? Do you know how poorly academic advisers are compensated by this government? Do you understand how my constant complaints to undergraduates about their use of plagiarism are a waste of my phenomenal talent?"

Her voice rose. "I deserve more than this. I should be running my own lab, not working for useless yes-men like Dr Eerie. He is half the academic I am, yet he's the one this wretched government turns to every time there's a bit of a leak of an unknown germ, a new variant of the common cold or a questionable strain of measles!"

Clarissa was shaking. "Basically, you've gone rogue?"

Toby waved a paw over the laptop. The keys began to lightly click by themselves.

"I'm a genius, Clarissa! I will write this up and present the paper at international conferences—and someone, somewhere, will offer me big bucks to do the research I've always wanted to do."

"But you're a witch! What about 'do no harm'?"

Raine's eyes grew sly. "If we don't know what causes harm, that's when we *do* harm," Raine replied.

"Gibberish!" spluttered Clarissa. "Complete nonsense. I'm going to tell the world what you did. The lives you put in danger."

Raine pushed the wand deeper into Old Pete's neck. He tried to twist away, but she grabbed his arm before turning back to Clarissa. "I don't think so, sweetheart. I'll tell you exactly what's going to happen here." She indicated the table where Toby now sat directly behind Clarissa's laptop. "I'm going to take your computer and your phone and your sweet, talking dog and disappear. But you and the old fella here, I'm afraid you're collateral damage."

Toby moved his paw over the mouse. It clicked on the send button. In the silence following Raine's last statement of intent, the click seemed loud.

Raine narrowed her eyes. "What are you doing?" She took the wand away from Old Pete's throat and aimed it at Toby.

Old Pete suddenly shrieked, clutching his chest, and collapsed into his chair. "My heart! My heart!"

Sparky set up a frantic barking. "Dad? Dad? Someone help him!"

Raine didn't know where to look first. As she

turned to Old Pete, Toby leapt from his chair and clamped his mouth around the hem of Clarissa's jeans, tugging her away. He knew Clarissa's instinct would be to rush to Mr Sharpy's aid, but Toby used every ounce of his strength to drag her backwards to the open patio doors. Once her brain began processing what was happening, Clarissa came willingly enough.

They chased around the side of the house, Clarissa oblivious to the fact that she was only wearing socks, and out into the front garden where the gate had been left open. To Clarissa's horror, she realised Raine hadn't arrived alone. Two sleek black cars were parked a little way along the road, far enough away from Mr Sharpy's house that nobody had heard them pulling up.

Now, as Clarissa and Toby paused, contemplating which way to run, the doors of the first car opened and two men in smart suits clambered out.

They were cutting off the road to town.

With nothing else for it, the decision was made. They headed left, into the village.

CHAPTER TWENTY-FIVE

Bushy Leaze, being a titchy village with maybe one hundred residents—if that—didn't have much to offer. Not even its own post office. It did have a pub, of course, where Mrs Crouch had taken shelter while Toby attended to the Master of Puppies, and a small shop, but that was about it.

Clarissa and Toby raced down the road, passing a bus shelter and an old red phone box that was now utilised as a library, neither of which lent themselves as good hiding places for a young woman and her dog. A swift glance back over his shoulder and Toby could see the suited men making ground on them.

Clarissa was struggling. She hadn't long been walking without a crutch, let alone running. Most nights her leg ached anyway, and now, as she sped along, she could already feel the pull.

"Look!" Clarissa pointed as they rounded a bend in the road. A little way beyond was a church, not much more than a chapel. "Maybe we can hide somewhere around there?"

Toby would have preferred to head away from Bushy Leaze and into the forest, but he wasn't sure how Clarissa would fare. "Let's hurry," he said, and they dashed across the road. Fumbling with the gate—a small iron affair that matched the height of the low retaining wall that ran around the church and its churchyard and only came up to mid-thigh—Clarissa finally managed to push it open. They rushed through and closed it behind them.

Panting loudly, Clarissa ducked behind the wall and semi-crawled towards the church. Reaching for the door handle—a sizable round brass ring—she twisted it. Locked.

"Oh, how very Christian!" she complained.

"Round the back," said Toby, whose acute hearing had picked out the sounds of their pursuers coming closer. Clarissa duck-walked after him until they were at the reverse of the stone building, then, catching her breath, pressed her back into the wall below a stained-glass window. "Poor Mr Sharpy!" she panted, her voice snuffly. "I should have found a way to help him—"

Toby, hearing a clanking, nudged her, interrupting her flow. "They're at the gate!"

"Now what?" Clarissa scanned their surroundings.

The churchyard, bathed in sunlight, sloped gently away from them. It was a pretty but tiddly affair. There were dozens rather than hundreds of graves, a few with flowers placed on them, dotted around among shrubs, mature trees and memorial benches, with good views out over the surrounding countryside. On this side of the village, the landscape opened out into farmland, fields of cows and sheep and cabbages.

There was nowhere to hide. Maybe the odd gravestone, but most of them were modest affairs. The only alternative was to throw themselves over the low retaining wall, but to what end?

"Have you found them?" Raine's voice, further away. "They can't have gone far!"

"They must be in here," one of the men responded. Too close.

"Clarissa?" Raine called, honing in on them. "Toby?"

Clarissa clamped her mouth shut, pressing harder against the wall as though she wished it would swallow them up.

"The old man's pegged it!" Raine shouted, almost gleefully. "That just leaves the pair of you. There's no way you're getting out of this."

Clarissa curled her lip.

"Give yourself up, Clarissa. If you do that, I'll spare the dog." She sounded nearby, as though she'd crept around the side of the church.

Toby growled, low in his throat. "Where you go, I go," he told Clarissa.

Clarissa pointed out a pair of headstones, leaning towards each other. "In that case ... Go!" she whispered.

Toby didn't need telling twice. He hurtled towards the headstone to the right, Clarissa on his tail, aiming for the one on the left. She drew her legs to her chest and slumped against it, the rough stone scratching her cheek. "I have to be honest, Toby. I'm not particularly good at attack and defence magick. I have no idea how to keep us safe!"

"Clarissa?" Raine wheedled.

Toby risked a peek. She was standing exactly where Clarissa had been just moments before, staring in their direction. She'd been joined by the two suited men. They stared blankly ahead, limited activity in their eyes. An enchantment, maybe? "You can't hide, my lovely. Come out now, and bring your lovely dog.

Let's put an end to this so I can carry on with the rest of my life."

"You're delusional," Clarissa called, remaining scrunched up behind her headstone. "You won't get away with it."

"I've been getting away with it for the past few weeks. Who's going to stop me?" Raine chuckled. "Not that pathetic Dr Eerie! And certainly not you!"

Toby poked his head out further, intentionally making the movement large enough so Raine would see him. "But I will."

"Toby!" Clarissa hissed, reaching for him.

Raine laughed, in a polite rather than amused fashion. "Bless your heart. You're a brave one. And a smart boy. I like that. You're wasted living with a journalist. Come with me and be *my* familiar, and together we'll make a million."

"I don't like money, I only like sammiches," Toby informed her. "I haven't had any lunch today, and that's making me cross."

"When we're finished here, I'll take you out for a steak dinner," Raine promised.

"Sounds good," said Toby. "Is it alright if my friends come?"

"Which friends?" Raine asked.

"These ones," said Toby and scratched hard at the

earth beneath him to forge deep lines. Then, sitting back so his weight was low around his rump, he lifted his soil-caked paws. "Blessed ancestors below, deeply sleeping in a row, nothing intricate and nothing fancy, hear my plea for necromancy!" he sang.

The earth began to shudder. Clarissa squeaked and rolled over onto her front. Clumps of soil and sods of grass flew into the air. She blinked, then squawked as a bony hand shot out of the grave directly below where she was lying. "Waaaah!" She scuttled backwards and collided with another headstone. It shattered around her, and another skeletal hand exploded into the open, swiftly followed by a head and the other arm.

"Toby? What are you doing?" Clarissa cried, scrambling backwards.

Toby remained where he was, paws conducting a skeletal band of warriors. "I'm playing Dr Clemence at her own game," he told her. "Let's see if she likes it."

As Clarissa inched towards him, dozens of skeletons began rising from the deep. Most of them had a covering of some kind—a shroud, tattered clothes, ceremonial garments—but in other cases, they were simply a collection of bones. Bones that clattered and clicked. Jaws that flapped or grinned. Skulls that pivoted this way and that.

Toby directed them up the slope towards Raine. She aimed her wand at them, firing indiscriminately. Unfortunately for her, in spite of her galactic-sized intellect, she hadn't allowed for the fact that it's impossible to *kill* skeletons. Any time she managed to hit one, it would collapse, then jerk around on the floor a little before rising once more and resuming its journey.

Raine backed away. "Get them!" she bellowed at her companions. One of the men lifted his arms as though he would fight them off, but the other took to his heels. On seeing his partner disappear around the side of the church, the first suit reconsidered and turned to go after him.

"No, no!" Toby said crossly, and waved a paw.

Nicely timed, the lead skeleton grabbed the suited man and, in one swift motion, bent his arm back. There was a loud crack and the suited man collapsed to the floor, writhing in agony and screaming for help.

Raine backed away. "Call them back, Clarissa!" she screamed, "Or I swear I'll raise an army of the undead to wipe out you and this entire village!"

Clarissa laughed. "Good luck with that! It's not me who's doing this!" She grinned at her faithful hound. "Go, Toby!"

Raine's eyes widened. "By himself?"

Toby, balancing neatly on his rump, directed the

lead skeleton with his right paw, making it advance, while, with his left paw, he bade a secondary skeleton to flank Raine.

Raine screamed again and cowered away, covering her head. "No! No!"

Bony fingers reached for her, two pairs of skeletal hands ... with more following. Toby played his battalion like a piano, darting a paw here, his snout there. Tiny skeletal finger bones stretched and tapped, reaching for Raine, a symphony of percussion.

"Enough."

A man, dressed head to toe in black, a cloak pulled low over his forehead, suddenly appeared at the corner of the church. He made a light gesture with his right hand. The skeletons halted, swaying back and forth, neither advancing nor retreating. He dropped his gaze to the suited man lying on the ground at his feet, and again waved his hand. The man became limp.

"Oh, thank you, thank you!" Raine cried. "They were going to kill me ... they were—"

"Dr Raine Clemence?" The strange man's voice remained soft and calm. "I'm here on behalf of the Ministry of Witches. I have been instructed to arrest you and accompany you to London for an audience with the Higher Council."

"You don't understand." Raine straightened up

and smoothed down her clothes. "I've done nothing. You should arrest these two!" She pointed at Toby. "He's a dark conjurer and a necromancer!"

The newcomer's head swivelled towards Toby. Toby saw the glow of his eyes beneath the brim of his hood. He couldn't tell for sure, but he thought there might have been a smile.

Turning his attention to Clarissa, he said, "I'm to apologise for any inconvenience you may have suffered and inform you that the Ministry of Witches will liaise with the mundane Home Office to bring an end to the current crisis. My superiors have asked whether they might call on you if they require some localised assistance?"

Taken aback, Clarissa nodded. "Well ... er ... of course. I'm not sure how I can be of any further assistance, but ... sure." She pointed at Toby. "But he's the one who should be thanked."

The mysterious man nodded and turned back. "And we do thank him. Good work, Toby. Good boy!"

CHAPTER TWENTY-SIX

With the skeletons safely back in their graves and Raine and her two suited strongarms escorted away by the mysterious man in black, Clarissa and Toby hurried back to Mr Sharpy's house, fully expecting to have to call an ambulance and the police to notify them of a sudden death.

But as Toby pushed the front door open and Clarissa limped in behind him, Mr Sharpy poked his head out of the kitchen. "Oh, there you are," he said. "Shall I put the kettle on?"

Clarissa reared back in surprise. "Is this your doing?" she asked Toby.

"Nope," said Toby, equally stunned.

Sparky, firmly cemented to his dad's slippers, beamed smugly at his friend.

"I beg your pardon?" Mr Sharpy cupped a hand to his ear.

"I thought you ... I mean ..." Clarissa gestured towards the living room. "You collapsed!"

"I faked it," Mr Sharpy said. "I hoped it might give you guys a chance to escape." He raised his eyebrows. "And it did, didn't it?"

Clarissa nodded. "Brilliant. Quite ... brilliant ... but Dr Clemence said you were dead."

"Pegged it, is what she said." Toby strived to be accurate.

"That's the interesting thing. Since I took ill, my pulse and my heart rate are sluggish, I've noticed. She tried for a pulse but she obviously didn't find one."

Clarissa clamped her hand on her heart. "I am so glad you're alright."

"The feeling's mutual, my friend. Now, tea?"

Toby left them to it. It occurred to him that while Clarissa was exchanging pleasantries with Old Pete, he had business to finish on Clarissa's laptop. He scurried into the living room and jumped onto a chair, then hurriedly set about creating a folder which, after altering the time and date stamp with a wiggle of a claw and a wriggle of a whisker, he saved to the cloud.

By the time Clarissa joined him at the table, mug of steaming tea in one hand and a plate of biscuits in the other, Toby was nonchalantly curled up on another chair, his eyebrows twitching.

"What are you up to?" Clarissa asked.

"Ever suspicious," he mumbled. "I'm just catching up on my sleep. It's been a long and tiring day."

Clarissa checked her inbox and spotted the read receipt from enquiries@ministryofwitches.co.uk. "You managed to send my email?"

"Thanks to Mr Sparky's diversion tactics," Toby told her. Credit where credit was due.

"I've been wondering how that MOW witch knew where to find us!"

"A jiggle here, a fidget there," Toby admitted. "I also sent it to Dr Eerie, just in case he's wondering where Dr Clemence has disappeared to."

"Naughty," said Clarissa, but she wasn't displeased and even snuck him a custard cream.

From somewhere in the depths of Clarissa's backpack, her phone began to ring. "Oooh!" She deposited her tea, sloshing it onto the table, and hurriedly scrambled among her belongings searching for the device. By the time she found it, it had fallen silent. "Unknown number," she lamented. "I hoped it would be—"

Toby didn't have a chance to find out who she hoped it would be because it began to ring again.

She frowned at the screen and answered. "Clarissa Page?"

"Ah, Ms Page!" a cheerful voice boomed. "So glad I've finally caught you. I'm Wizard Bracken Goldbird from the Ministry of Witches Higher Council—"

"Gosh!" Clarissa put a hand to her throat. Toby leaned in to listen.

"We wanted to thank you for the work you put into apprehending Raine Clemence. She's been under investigation for some time because we had our suspicions, but we've lacked the evidence to take our inquiries any further. I can't divulge too much, but the woman is a fraud from start to finish. She has a third-class degree from some dubious overseas online university, and she bought her MSc and PhD certificates."

"Really?" Clarissa thought about Raine's self-assurance when bigging up her abilities, her confidence when interacting with Dr Eerie.

"Oh yes."

"You know she was intending to sell the results of this experiment?" Clarissa asked. "She said it could be used as a weapon!"

"We assumed that to be the case. She's been in league with some particularly shady characters. Fortunately, we think we know the source of the leak for this particular virus. The original specimen had been stored in a Ukrainian wizard's lab, but, with the invasion and one thing and another, it had to be moved. We've now ensured it's being kept in a vault far away from prying eyes or greasy fingers."

Clarissa nodded, her journalist's brain kicking in. She pulled her notebook towards her and picked up a pen. "I'm thrilled to hear that."

Wizard Goldbird's tone became delicate. "With regards to the way forward with Sun Valley's infected—"

"Yes?" Clarissa's pen hovered above a page.

"While I can't be more specific, I'd like to assure you that this particular strain of zombie virus is one of the milder versions. It tends to attach to those who are immunocompromised in the first place—the elderly, for example."

"I see. That would explain why I didn't catch it," Clarissa said. "And why those who did, tended to be older."

"We will now work with the government to ensure control and containment to eradicate the outbreak, but we want to go further than that." Wizard Goldbird cleared his throat. "It would be an immeasurable service on your part if you could assist us with curing the sick?"

"Well, ah, I'm not a nurse." *Far from it*, thought Clarissa.

"But you can make them well," Toby interrupted.

"Shhh!" Clarissa flapped her hand at him.

"But you can!"

"Wizard Goldbird, all I did was give the two zombies I interacted with cups of tea and paracetamol," Clarissa explained. "Anyone can do that!"

"It's not ordinary tea, though," Toby interspersed.

"It is, Toby, shhhh!" Clarissa reached out to push him off the chair. "It's tea with milk. That's all it is!"

"It's tea with milk *and* stirred with a spell," Toby told her.

"Huh?" Clarissa changed her mind and grabbed hold of his collar instead of pushing him away.

"When you stir it! The song you sing or hum? It's a spell!"

"The one my mum used to sing to me?" Clarissa's mouth dropped open as realisation dawned.

Wizard Goldbird prompted her. "What do you think, Clarissa? If we set up a mobile kitchen at the building site, would you be able to lead on this project? A zombie mission? Make urns full of tea? We'll supply paracetamol too, cases of them, and send down bodies—"

"Bodies?" Clarissa cringed at that.

"Sorry, I meant *people*, to assist you."

Clarissa's jaw dropped. She would lead a mission? People would be looking to her to command and make decisions. Could she do that?

She glanced at Toby. He grinned his big, wide, toothy dog smile.

She thought back to the last time she'd been at Boyd's building site, the place crawling with soldiers in gas masks carrying huge guns. "No harm will come to those who are infected, will it?"

"You have my word."

She nodded, even though Wizard Goldbird couldn't see her. "Very well. I'm going to need portable showers and lots of clean clothes to give out to people. And some hairdressers and barbers, perhaps?"

"We can do all that," Wizard Goldbird confirmed. "I'll have my assistant contact you, and he'll get straight on it. Check your email."

"Will do," said Clarissa.

"Thank you, Clarissa. And thank you, Toby!" Wizard Goldbird said, and hung up.

"Get us!" exclaimed Toby, wobbling his head. "Making our mark with the Ministry of Witches."

"Don't start being all fat-headed," Clarissa warned him, nudging her computer mouse. "It's most unbecoming." She cocked her head, scanning her email and spotting something unexpected. "What's this?"

Toby leaned over to sneak a peek at the little yellow file that had popped up on her screen. "I have no idea," he said, and snuggled back down on his seat.

Clarissa opened the file. "It's a bit of film. I must have missed it the first time. Yes. See, the date and time stamp are—" She caught her breath. A moment later she caught it again, her shoulders pulling back and her eyes widening.

"What a total jerk!" She grunted and slapped the lid of her laptop down. "What an absolute pillock! Let's pack up, Toby. We're going home!"

EPILOGUE

"What do you think, Toby?" Old Pete asked. "Not bad, eh?"

According to Sparky, when Old Pete had been Young Pete, he'd been a dab hand at DIY. He still had all his tools in a large store in his garden, and when Clarissa had mentioned Toby's wizard shack to him, he'd offered to come and help sort the interior out.

There were things that Old Pete seemed quite good at—the shack now had a chipboard floor, ready to be carpeted, and some wall lining—but he wasn't very good with stepladders, so the uppermost bookcases were a weeny bit crooked.

As Moriarty was quick to point out. "I've seen straighter circles, to be fair," she said.

Toby gave her a look, and Moriarty turned her attention to her right paw instead.

"How are you getting on, Mr Sharpy?" Ed stuck his head around the shed door. He was outside, painting the shack a beautiful shiny midnight blue. When it was dry, he'd promised Toby that he'd use stencils to paint a galaxy of stars and planets.

Toby was thrilled. He'd decided against green in the end because midnight blue complemented his fur so much more, and green reminded him of smelly zombies! All he needed to do now was persuade Mrs Crouch to make him some curtains and have Old Pete hang some of Toby's prized photos on the walls, and he could move in! He couldn't wait.

He skipped outside to survey Ed's work. Ed balanced easily on the ladder, applying some finishing touches to a couple of areas he'd missed before. The paintwork gleamed, although a few insects had unfortunately become stuck and would now be forever immortalised among the stars.

Oops. Sorry about that, thought Toby.

"So what happened to Clarissa's other beau?" Moriarty asked. "I've not seen him around. Did you tell her he has a wife?"

"I didn't want to be so blunt," Toby said. "It seemed unnecessarily mean. I wanted her to find out for herself. I took steps to ensure she'd never want to see him again," said Toby the Dogfather.

Moriarty purred. "How did you manage that?"

"A little AI."

She wrinkled her nose. "Ay-eye? What's that?"

"A dot I. Artificial intelligence."

"Ah, something that's peculiar to dogs, is it?" Moriarty asked.

Toby rolled his eyes. "It's like computer software."

Moriarty was none the wiser. She stifled a yawn.

"No, really. It's quite clever," Toby insisted. "I used existing images of Connor from his social media profiles and I artificially generated a video of him walking along outside the building site down town on the night of the jamboree."

"So?" Moriarty refused to be impressed.

"Well, I couldn't find any photos of him and his wife, and I should imagine that's in no way coincidental ... so I took steps to ... er ... persuade Clarissa of the truth. I artificially generated a woman to walk alongside him."

"Okay." Moriarty nodded her approval. "And that put your hooman off?"

Toby shrugged. "That and the fact he was pushing a baby in a buggy."

"You ..? Wha ...? I never said he had kittens!"

Moriarty chuckled. “Yeah, that would put me off, too.” She narrowed her eyes. “Sneaky.”

“And ... I added a child tagging along behind them. Erm ... three children, in fact. All under five.”

“Wow,” said Moriarty. “I’d hate to end up on the wrong side of you.”

“It did the trick.” Toby grinned. “It made DC Ed a much better proposition.”

“Tea up!” Clarissa came out of the house carrying a tray with a teapot and mugs. “Tea for the workers!” she sang, setting the tray down on the garden table.

Mr Sharpy quickly downed tools and came out of the shack, stretching his back and fingers. “I could murder a cuppa!”

Ed pulled a face. “Please don’t use the *M* word.”

Clarissa laughed. “It’s not as though you’ve been working any murder cases lately. You’ve had a bit of a break.”

“True.” Ed had been assisting another team with their enquiries into Travis Boyd’s nefarious activities. The buying and selling of land without the requisite permits. The fact that his workers had disturbed several forgotten graves. The fact that they had strived to dispose of those bodies without recourse to the appropriate authorities. The fact that they had left human remains exposed to the elements for days.

No wonder the receptionist had been so shady.

And that would explain how Debbie had come across Mary Elizabeth Salcombe's tiara.

Ed's hunch was that the council knew about Boyd's activities and had been covering up for him. There was every chance a department higher up the chain—perhaps even in Westminster—knew what was going on but hadn't taken any action.

Ed shrugged. It would all come out in the wash. "You've been working hard, too!"

Clarissa nodded. She'd been employed long hours down at the building site, which had become a makeshift field hospital for those suffering from the zombie virus. "Everyone seems to be making an excellent recovery. As of this morning, the last of them has been allowed home. We'll have some nurses going in and checking on them regularly, and I've offered to make flasks of tea for anyone who suffers a relapse, but I'm hopeful we're through the worst."

"Well done, you!" Ed clambered down from his ladder.

"It's nothing," said Clarissa. "I'm just happy I could help. Anyone can make tea and say a few kind words." The added bonus was that she could report the whole story in *The Celestine Times*, and she'd made it to the front cover on three successive days. Her career was picking up.

He threw an arm around her. "You're amazing!"

"Oh!" She pushed him away. "You're not getting me covered in paint, are you? Awww!" She dabbed at some blue he'd transferred to her t-shirt.

"You can hardly see it!" Ed protested. "It'll wash out."

"It definitely won't," Toby remarked.

"He doesn't know much about paint, does he?" Moriarty asked.

Clarissa stared slyly at Ed. "It's a good job I like you."

He beamed. "I like you, too."

Moriarty pretended to cough up a hairball.

"Cwooooooarrh!"

Everyone froze.

"Cwooooooarrh!"

Old Pete turned his head. The sound had come from over the other side of Clarissa and Toby's garden fence.

"Is that Mrs Crouch?" Ed whispered.

"I reckon so." Clarissa frowned. "Toby? You'll have to do the honours."

Toby bounded up the wizard shack's staircase and onto the platform from where he had a good view into

Mrs Crouch's garden. He could see her rubbing her throat as she trimmed back a rose bush. "Mrs Crouch?" he called. "Mrs Crouch? Would you like to come round for a cuppa? We're finishing my shed!"

Mrs Crouch peered up at him. "Are you? That would be lovely, Toby, thank you, but I'm not sure I'm feeling too well."

"Don't you worry about a thing, Mrs Crouch!" Toby called back, his tail wagging with enthusiasm. "We'll have you right in no time!"

Clarissa smiled at Ed and handed him the teapot so he could pour for Mr Sharpy. "I'd better put the kettle on again," she said.

COMING SOON

Fancy reading more of Toby's adventures?

Born to be Styled

Spellbound Hound Magic and Mystery Book 6

Toby is a pooch in need of a short back and sides.

Unfortunately, an unscheduled appointment at Toby's local poodle parlour proves particularly perilous for the poor proprietor.

Both she, and her poor poodle, are left pining.

But when you have a spellbound hound on the case, it turns out murder can be stylish after all!

Available to preorder on Amazon.

Up, Pup and Away

Spellbound Hound Magic and Mystery Book 7

Toby's been building up quite a reputation for himself. Well, he likes to think so.

It's therefore no surprise that when things go wrong for any of his canine friends, he gets called in to help them out. Lost puppies? No problem! Dognapping victim? Piece of cake.
There's no mystery that our intrepid hound won't try and solve.

But this time it's personal.

COMING SOON

The Pointy Woman is back … and Toby has a rather large bone to pick with her.

Available for preorder on Amazon.

ALSO BY JEANNIE WYCHERLEY

Spellbound Hound

(*in reading order*)

Ain't Nothing but a Pound Dog: Spellbound Hound Magic and Mystery Book 1

A Curse, a Coven and a Canine: Spellbound Hound Magic and Mystery Book 2

Bark Side of the Moon: Spellbound Hound Magic and Mystery Book 3

Master of Puppies: Spellbound Hound Magic and Mystery Book 4

Dem Bones, Dem Bones: Spellbound Hound Magic and Mystery Book 5

Born to be Styled: Spellbound Hound Magic and Mystery Book 6 (Release Feb 2024)

Up, Pup and Away: Spellbound Hound Magic and Mystery Book 7 (Release April 2024)

The Complete Wonky Inn Series

(*in reading order*)

The Wonkiest Witch: Wonky Inn Book 1

The Ghosts of Wonky Inn: Wonky Inn Book 2

Weird Wedding at Wonky Inn: Wonky Inn Book 3

The Witch Who Killed Christmas: Wonky Inn Christmas Special

Fearful Fortunes and Terrible Tarot: Wonky Inn Book 4

The Mystery of the Marsh Malaise: Wonky Inn Book 5

The Mysterious Mr Wylie: Wonky Inn Book 6

The Great Witchy Cake Off: Wonky Inn Book 7

Vengeful Vampire at Wonky Inn: Wonky Inn Book 8

Witching in a Winter Wonkyland: A Wonky Inn Christmas Cozy Special

A Gaggle of Ghastly Grandmamas: Wonky Inn Book 9

Magic, Murder and a Movie Star: Wonky Inn Book 10

O' Witchy Town of Whittlecombe: A Wonky Inn Christmas Cozy Special

Judge, Jury and Jailhouse Rockcakes: Wonky Inn Book 11

A Midsummer Night's Wonky: Wonky Inn Book 12

Halloween Heebie-Geebies: Wonky Inn Book 13

Owl I want for Witchmas is Hoo: A Wonky Inn Christmas Cozy Mystery

Oh Mummy!: Wonky Inn Book 14

Pieces of Hate: Wonky Inn Book 15

The Faery of Witchmas Past: A Wonky Inn Christmas Cozy Special

Wonkytonk Witch: A Wonky Inn Mystery

A Wonky Apprentice: Wonky Inn Book 17

A Barbarous Band of Blood Brothers: Wonky Inn Book 18 (Release date TBC)

Wonderland Detective Agency

Dead as a Dodo: Wonderland Detective Agency Book 1

The Rabbit Hole Murders: Wonderland Detective Agency Book 2

Tweedledumb and Tweedledie: Wonderland Detective Agency Book 3

The Curious Incident at the Pig and Pepper: Wonderland Detective Agency Book 4

A Tragic Tea Party: Wonderland Detective Agency Book 5

The Pool of Tears: Wonderland Detective Agency Book 6

Into the Labyrinth: Wonderland Detective Agency Book 7 (Release TBC)

The Municipality of Lost Souls

Midnight Garden: The Extra Ordinary World Novella Series Book 1

Beyond the Veil

Crone

A Concerto for the Dead and Dying

Deadly Encounters: A collection of short stories

Keepers of the Flame: A love story

With Peter Alderson Sharp

The Creature from the Grim Mire: A humorous Sci-fi, Time Travel and Alien Contact Mystery

Non-Fiction

Losing my best Friend

Thoughtful support for those affected by dog bereavement or pet loss

Follow Jeannie Wycherley

Buy me a coffee

www.buymeacoffee.com/jeanniewych

Find out more at on the website www.jeanniewycherley.co.uk

Or visit her on Facebook for her fiction

www.facebook.com/jeanniewycherley

Follow Jeannie on Instagram (for bears and books) www.instagram.com/jeanniewycherley

See Jeannie on Tiktok @jeanniewycherley

Sign up for Jeannie's newsletter on her website www.subscribepage.com/JeannieWycherleyWonky

Printed in Great Britain
by Amazon

35340379R00189